FROM AVON BOOKS—
THE MAGNIFICENT SEA ADVENTURES
OF TRISTAN JONES

THE INCREDIBLE VOYAGE
"A unique chronicle...Lusty, rough-talking, full of harrowing interludes."

Wall Street Journal

ICE!
"A nail-biting tale...Rich in history, irrepressible wit and salty excitement."

US Magazine

SAGA OF A WAYWARD SAILOR
"At the core of Jones' book is his fundamental belief in the value of personal freedom, no matter what the hardship, no matter what weaknesses are exposed."

Chicago Tribune Book World

ADRIFT
"Tristan Jones is something else...brash and irreverent but with a certain humanness and warmth."

Houston Post

NOW...
AKA
"A lyrical and intelligent account of both man and dolphin and the relationship they have to the sea and to each other...This book is a requirement for Jones' fans and for those who have yet to cruise the world with Jones."

Library Journal

Other Avon Books by
Tristan Jones

ADRIFT
ICE!
THE INCREDIBLE VOYAGE
SAGA OF A WAYWARD SAILOR

TRISTAN JONES

AVON
PUBLISHERS OF BARD, CAMELOT, DISCUS AND FLARE BOOKS

AVON BOOKS
A division of
The Hearst Corporation
1790 Broadway
New York, New York 10019

The Macmillan Publishing Co., Inc. edition contains the
following Library of Congress Cataloging in Publication Data:

   Jones, Tristan, 1924-
    Aka.

    I. Title.
   PR6060.059A77 1981   823'.914   81-7279
                                 AACR2

First Avon Printing, September, 1983

Printed in the U.S.A.

OP 10 9 8 7 6 5 4 3 2 1

To *Dagon*, for the dolphins, that they may be spared further slaughter by man.

Da cael ynys mor mawr.
(It is good to find an island in an ocean.)
Cyrys ar Yale (Welsh bard) *The Red Book of Talgarth* (A.D. 1400).

Antigua, Guadaloupe, Santo Domingo, Copenhagen, and Manhattan, January–December 1980.

(Dagon was the main god of the Philistines, and later of the Phoenicians. He was represented with the upper part of a man and the tail of a dolphin.)

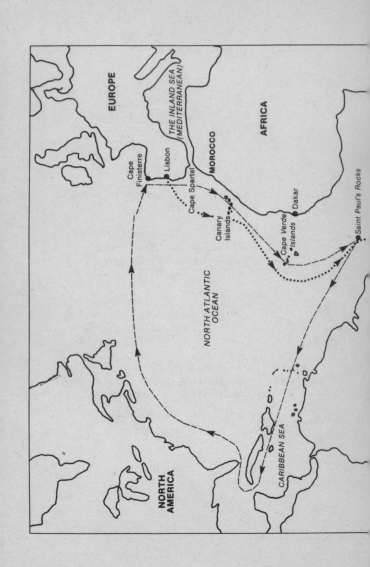

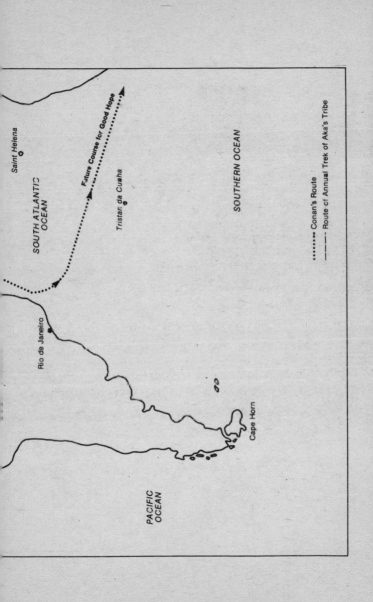

Contents

Foreword

THIS STORY is not told only for ocean-yacht-racing enthusiasts, nor only for experts, nor only for perfectionists in any field.

My tale is told also for those who have never stepped on board an ocean-sailing vessel, who have never known the elation of running free before the wind under a star-laden sky, who have rarely seen our wonderful relatives, the mammals of the sea, except in captivity.

If my tale can bring to people ashore a little of the joy, a little of the elation and wonder, and even a mite of the pain and suffering that voyagers and other mammals know at sea, then any carping of pierhead critics will be to this book as the squeaks of an unoiled sheet-block are to a vessel safely at anchor in her own quiet haven.

Acknowledgments

TO Professor Charles H. Hapgood, author of *Maps of the Ancient Sea Kings* (E. P. Dutton)

To Surgeon Commander F. St. C. Golden, Royal Navy, senior medical officer (survival medicine), Institute of Naval Medicine, Alverstoke, England, for valuable information on the effects of immersion of a human in seawater for a prolonged period

To Lieutenant Colonel Peter Thomas, Royal Marines (Ret.), Secretary, Royal Naval Sailing Association, Portsmouth, England, for his patience and assistance in making valuable contacts.

To International Marine Paint Company, New Jersey, for information on cupreous traces in seawater.

To the members of the Atlantic Society, for their faith in the past and hope for the future.

To the survivors of the last warship of the World War II Polish navy, who lent me the hallowed name of their ship, *Blytskwtska*; for their superb examples in gallantry.

Part 1: Departure

Tursiops truncatus, a subspecies of the family Delphinidae, of the order Cetacea, is known to sailors as the bottle-nosed dolphin. In North America some landsmen call them the "common porpoise."

Chapter 1

THE LONGEST AKA'S DOLPHIN TRIBE ever stays in one area is when
the females give birth. All through their history, as long as the legends
of their Wise Ones reached back, their calves had been born in the warm
waters that wash the two lonely rocks in the equatorial mid-Atlantic.

Aka and the Wise Ones, in the tale-telling times, transmit holographic
images to the rest of the 143 bottle-nosed dolphins in the tribe of how
their home had once been, before the seas rose and covered all but the
two tiny islets, the very top of the highest peak of the beautiful land that
had been Atlantis, the home-island of the Sea Kings. The Atlanteans had
been different from modern Man, "say" the Wise Ones. True, they had
fished, but they had never harmed or purposely murdered the dolphins.
On the contrary, the Sea Kings had learned to communicate with them,
and had included the dolphins in their pantheon of gods, and in return
the dolphins had herded the fish for the Atlanteans and accompanied
the Sea Kings on their voyages of trade and exploration.

Eventually, after eons of time, the waters had swiftly risen and it had
been time for the last of the Sea Kings to leave once-lovely Atlantis in
the warm seas. On their long graceful ships with purple sails the Sea
Kings had figureheads of dolphins cast in gold, and as they hauled their
anchors for the last time their high priest had made a vow that when
they reached their new home in the inland sea, they would raise a tem-

ch would be the new center of the world and they would name
nonor of their sea gods. *Eh-ee*, the name of the temple, had come
vn in the dolphin legends through twelve thousand years and twelve
1ousand treks around the North Atlantic Ocean. It was the closest the
dolphins could come to pronouncing the human word *Delphi*.

Each August, when the calves are two to three months old, the dolphins of Aka's tribe leave the lonely rocks, now known to humans as St.
Paul's, and make their way, by taste and their guiding stars, into the
west-flowing Guinea Current, warm after its long traipse up the west
African coast. They do not hurry. The fish scouts and the shoal herders
range up to a hundred miles either side of the main body of 112 dolphins. After two months in the warm Guinea Current, they join the
North Equatorial Current, which flows down the coast of Africa from
the north and swings west across the ocean to the West Indies. The tribe
roams around the West Indies Islands for three months; there the fish
abound from October to December. Then it is time to move northeast,
into the Gulf Stream. It takes the tribe four months to make its way east
across the North Atlantic, ranging north almost as far as Iceland, to
their traditional landfall of Cape Finisterre, the northwest tip of Spain.
From then on, as they continue south, is their mating time, from Finisterre to the Moroccan coast.

From Finisterre, the dolphins steadily make their way south during
March and April, south in the cool Portugal current, in a vast area
which extends right down the coast of Portugal, across the herring, cod,
and pilchard-teeming Straits of Gibraltar, right down to the coast of
Mauritania, where the shoals of mullet darken the oceans like undersea
clouds. They do not swim along in a direct route, but range as far west
as Madeira and the Canary Islands, and sometimes they even visit into
the Mediterranean as far east as the Balearic Islands and Corsica; but,
by their ancient law, no further.

By mid-April each year the tribe has plowed its way through the Cape
Verde Islands and, always with several females heavy with calf from the
previous year's mating, heads southwest by south, right across the Guinea Current again, in a line as straight as an arrow, guided as always by
their taste and the stars, back to the two lonely warm islets and the safe
inlet, which is all that remains of Atlantis, which has always been their
ancestral home, ever since the dawning of their recorded history twenty
million years ago.

Conan reread the telegram, picked up the phone, and as he dialed, re-

minded himself not to mention the name *Josephine*. Outside,
York traffic roared.

"Ruth," he said in a slight Scottish burr, "I want to see you urge
... no, I don't want to discuss it on the phone ... I have to go away f.
a while ..."

He listened for a moment, then he said, "Okay, Formelli's then, at sev-
en." He waited for another minute, listening. Then he smiled and murmured, "I love you, too," and hung up the phone.

Conan picked up the cable again and scanned it. His hand shook as
he read it, then he groaned quietly to himself and let the cable fall onto
his desk. He was in corduroy pants and shirt sleeves. He was of medium
build, sinewy yet not thin, with thinning dark hair and trimly shaped
graying beard. He held his head slightly thrust forward, as if he were
sniffing the air. His gray eyes were now half-closed in shock and
sorrow.

For a few minutes he stared out of his fifth-floor apartment window
at the Seventh Avenue traffic rumbling below. As Conan stood at the
window he held both feet planted apart, as if he were on the deck of a
ship at sea. Every move he made, even as he turned his head to look
along the avenue, was as decisive as if it had been considered before-
hand. He had the look of a man who is accustomed to making up his
mind and acting upon his decision—the kind of man whose obvious inner strength is, when all is well, resented by weaker beings. He was the
rare kind of person who was disbelieved in by those who had no inkling
of the furnace in which Conan's strength had been forged.

In his mind's eye, Conan saw *Josephine* and Shaughnessy again as he
had two years previously: *Josephine* shapely and trim, sleek as ever;
Shaughnessy, a grinning, bald wiry leprechaun, burned by the ocean
sun. It had been at Annapolis, at the town quay. Shaughnessy had just
anchored the forty-four-foot sloop after a four-thousand-mile passage
from England, cleared U.S. Customs, and had rowed ashore to meet
Conan again for the first time in six years.

He and Shaughnessy had drunk the afternoon away together at a
crowded bar on the waterfront. On principle neither of them drank at
sea and Shaughnessy had been thirty-two days dry, Conan remembered.
He picked up the cable again, read it, sighed, and looked around his tiny,
grubby, too expensive apartment, at the tatty furniture, most of it sal-
vaged from the street. His gaze wandered over the piles of books on the
floor and he glared for a few seconds at the half-finished book-type-
script, which, like a greedy, insatiable stepchild, sat accusingly on his
desk. Conan took another quick glance at the cable:

NESSY KILLED ACCIDENT STOP QUERY CAN YOU SKIP-
LOOP JOSEPHINE LISBON GLOBE AROUND WORLD RACE
MMENCES SECOND APRIL REPLY URGENTEST STOP MIKE
HOUGHTON.

Conan picked up the phone.

"Western Union," he said after a few seconds. "Yes, a cable . . . inter-national . . . to England . . . Mike Houghton, Southern Counties Ocean Cruising Club, Sandleston . . ." Conan spelled out the name of the town for the operator. "England . . . the text of the message is 'yes stop arrive Lisbon Friday twenty-seventh March stop Bill Conan.' "

Then he headed for his travel agent's office.

When Conan arrived at Formelli's restaurant it was six-forty. The place was not yet packed. He ordered a Watney's Red Barrel beer—For-melli's stocked brews from several different countries. Conan looked around the restaurant. Most of the customers were young people who, Conan guessed, were students, but there were a few older people, mostly men, regulars, who always seemed to be either reading or writing as they ate. Conan supposed that they, too, were writers, though there was no way he could know for sure. Most people tended to keep to them-selves in Manhattan, even in Greenwich Village.

While he waited for his beer, Conan looked around the restaurant and noted a couple of good-looking girls. He delved into his inside jacket pocket, brought out the airline tickets, and inspected them. He started to make mental notes on the clothes and other gear he would need to take with him. Suddenly, as if startled, he looked up, his head turned to-ward the restaurant doorway.

There are magic moments in the lives of lovers. For some they are rare, for others not. Suddenly, for no obvious reason, there is an aware-ness, a private certainty, that the *other* is close by, no matter what the time or place, nor how many other people may be present. There is a quickening of the senses; colors brighten, noises soften, shapes sharpen, life is kinder, strangers tend to fade into an amorphous background that is all their own. Suddenly, almost involuntarily, and yet perhaps not, one's head turns, one's pulse quickens, one's eyes focus, and there is one's beloved. So it was, at precisely three minutes to seven in the eve-ning, in the crowded restaurant, between Bill Conan and Ruth Fleming, he sitting at a wall table at the far inner end of the room, and she peer-ing over the shoulders of recent arrivals waiting around the doorway for a table.

Conan smiled as Ruth edged her way past the coterie at the entrance, her eyes fixed on Conan all the while, and made her way to him. He started to rise, she shook her head.

Conan glanced at his wristwatch. "Early," he said. It was a private joke between them. He reached for the parcel she was carrying and put it beside his chair.

"Don't drop my skates, Conan," she said. Her voice was husky and low. She leaned over the corner of the table and lightly brushed his beard with her lips.

She was three inches shorter than Conan, about five feet eight, but her slenderness made her appear taller. She looked to be in her middle twenties, and only the self-assured grace with which she opened her gray coat and shucked it over her shoulders for Conan to take from her gave any indication of her true age of thirty-four.

She wore her natural ash-blond hair shoulder length. Her face was peculiarly American—middle American. It was a mite too long to be considered classical. Her cheekbones were high enough to be German, yet her green eyes and brow were purely Irish, while her nose, very slightly patrician, and her complexion, were straight out of the English Home Counties. As her head moved and the light touched and defined the planes and angles of her facial structure, so, to Conan's eyes, she seemed to change into, and back from, and yet again into, three different women, while always remaining the same person. Both the roaming sailor and the writer in Conan were well aware of the quicksilver alchemy of Ruth's appearance. As he watched her sit, he remembered how sometimes, in the companionable moments after they had made love, he told her long, rambling, fanciful tales about her ancestry, and she laughed softly and held him closer to her. Those were the rare moments when the hard veneer which her ten years in New York City had imposed on her dissolved and her almost-naive middle-western innocence—openness might be a better way to think of it, Conan thought—was exposed.

"So what's happening?" Ruth asked quietly. She placed a hand on Conan's arm. She wore a tailored suit, gray with green trimmings, for work at the bank office during the week.

Conan reached into his pocket, extracted the cable, and passed it to her.

Ruth quickly donned a pair of fashionably oversized glasses, and read it, twice. She tried to stop herself from saying, "And you've accepted." It was a flat statement.

"There really wasn't time to discuss—I had to get a cable away fast, so that Houghton would get it in time . . ." He trailed off meekly. His accent had the soft brogue of a northern Briton who has been most of his life at sea, but after four years in the States, Conan's vowels were beginning to flatten out American style.

"How long's the race?" Ruth asked in a small voice, as she replaced the glasses in her purse.

"It's the Sunday Globe race. . . . There's a fifty-thousand-pound prize—"

Ruth broke in, as a waitress, a young "resting" actress, arrived to take their orders. "What's that in real money?" She was smiling.

By the time the waitress had left, Conan had done the calculation. "A hundred and eighteen thousand dollars . . . that's the prize," he said, as he lifted his beer glass. He thought of the other prizes—the visions, the obscurities, the revelations; the profundity, the finality of the sea, the way in which the sea renders remote the cares and wastes of the land. That, to Conan, was the greatest of her prizes—the one worth all the discomforts, the perils and dangers the sea so slyly hid from the unwary.

Ruth was silent. For a moment she drummed her fingers on the table and stared at Conan. She reflected on the way his soul seemed to stir in his eyes when he looked at her, and how they changed to granite when he did not; how the light and warmth left when he looked around him, away from her.

She said, "But what about your writing, Bill? You've written four books since you came to New York. . . . You're becoming better known. . . . Why do you have to go on this stupid race? How long is it for, anyhow?"

Conan finished his beer. He firmly placed the glass on the table and looked directly into Ruth's eyes. "It's round the world, nonstop, Lisbon to Lisbon," he said. His tone was boyishly defensive.

There was dead silence between them for a full minute. Ruth opened her mouth slightly as she stared at Conan. She winced and said, "Say that again, Conan . . . slowly. My adrenaline is getting in my ears."

Conan regarded her without expression for a moment. He started to say, "Round the—" His voice was hoarse. He cleared his throat.

"Yes, come on, Bill."

"It's a tremendous chance for me to . . ." He hesitated.

"Prove yourself?" Ruth asked quietly, sharply. "Jesus Christ, Conan, you're fifty-six years old. You've just about done everything. You've proved yourself time and again. All your life you've been proving yourself. What was it . . . ordinary seaman to lieutenant, Royal bloody Navy. . . ?"

"Please, Ruth," Conan murmured as the waitress set their plates on the table. There was a silence until the waitress left. Ruth picked up her fork. She left her knife on the table, as Americans do, until she needed it.

Quietly she said, "All that time at sea . . . in small sailing boats . . . how many years was it?"

"Twenty-two . . . and fourteen in the service . . ."

"And you still haven't had enough?"

"That was mostly delivery trips," he said. "This race is something really special . . ." Again his voice trailed off.

There was another painful silence between them.

Ruth thought of how, after almost two decades of disappointment, she had at last found a man whom she could respect as well as truly love. She envisioned, vaguely, the faces of her ex-husband and some of her previous lovers, but they were mere blurs in her consciousness. For the most they had been either childish, vain, or jealous. To her, Bill Conan had more personality, more intelligence, and certainly more good humor and affection in his little finger than the rest had among them.

Conan felt again the hopelessness of the years he had been alone; a creeping inner coldness, the old orphaning. As he looked at Ruth he wished to God he could take her with him. That was impossible. That he loved her—well and truly loved her, to the depths of his soul—there was not, in his whole being, a shard of doubt. That he needed her was self-evident, the stirring of his mind and groin informed him as he looked at her. Besides, she was his friend.

"What about us, Conan?" Ruth finally asked.

Conan laid down his knife and fork and took a swig of beer, his eyes fixed all the while on hers. He wiped his lips with his napkin and leaned slightly toward her. "It's only for a few short months, Ruth. . . . Just this one last time. . . . I'm drying up . . . I'm writing less and less every day. They don't want to know about real people in real situations. They want . . ." he hesitated, then almost breathed the quotes around the word " 'romance' and they don't see that the real romance is in reality . . . the way things really are."

He looked briefly away from her around the restaurant. He stared for a moment at two males, both, he guessed, in their mid-thirties, one bearded, the other heavily mustachioed, both dressed in black leather caps and jackets, both heavily festooned with chains, both with eyes like lost children. She followed his gaze, then their eyes met again. She smiled. Conan looked away from her again, to where three blank-eyed youths, two of them with their hair longer than Ruth's were making their way to a table.

Suddenly, one of the youths, big and heavy and, thought Conan, fed for most of his few years on prime Texas beef, noticed Conan watching him. The boy glared at him in sullen hostility, a look that swiftly took in Conan's graying beard and glared in the arrogance that is a common intuitive reaction of much American youth toward older people. Conan, for a split second, thought of some of the lads he had sailed with over the years; then, just as fast as the remembrances had come, so, as he turned back to Ruth, they dissolved.

Ruth said, "Is it the danger, Conan?"

He looked at her steadily for a moment. Then he said, "Partly . . . there's that, too. But I have to be independent, Ruth. I suppose it's the way I was brought up. It may be considered old-fashioned here and now, but I just don't ever want to have to be in the situation of having possibly to ask you"—or any woman, he thought—"for anything. . . ."

"How long is this race, anyway?" she asked him.

Conan's face brightened. He took out his small notebook and consulted it. "Well, let's see," he said. He leafed through the pages. "Yes, here we are. Chichester did it in nine months back in sixty-six and sixty-seven . . . and Alex Rose did it in a year . . . Knox-Johnston in almost eleven months . . ." Conan grinned at Ruth. ". . . and Chay Blythe did it the wrong way round in just over nine months in seventy-one."

"Well, bully for Captain Blythe," said Ruth.

"Looks like it'll be around ten months," observed Conan.

There was a silence between them for what seemed to Conan to be an eternity. Then Ruth said, "You're mad, Conan. You know that?" She put her hand on his arm. "But I love you, you crazy, off-the-wall limey!"

"Then it's all right with you, Ruth? Okay with you? You can get away from the office and come to Lisbon with me?"

"No, it's not all right, Conan, and you goddamwell know it, and yes, I'll come . . ." She withdrew her hand from his arm. ". . . and I might *just* be here when you get back, *if* you get back to New York." There was a pause for a few seconds, then she said, "A year, a whole goddam year!" Quickly she finished her coffee. "Why do you do it, Conan? Don't you know, can't you get it into that stupid Scottish head of yours that the time for heroes is long gone? Why the hell couldn't you be a—an advertising agent, for God's sake, or—or—a—a taxi driver?"

Conan glanced momentarily at the old half-model hulls on the wall, their varnish now dulled with years of exposure to the steam and smoke of the restaurant. Phrases flashed through his head (the subtlety, the flexibility, the *mystery* of sail—the infinite variety and the incalculable complexity of the forces that are harnessed to serve the sailor's purpose: the wayward wind that resists all mastery, the would-be bitch sea, the frail, fierce phantom which is the ship herself, and which is always something more than the sum of her myriad parts. Her power, at the same time restraining and urgent—the sleek, reluctant beauty of her hull under the dominion of the mute sails she wears. . .).

Conan looked at Ruth. He smiled at her. "It'll keep me off the booze," he said. "Come on, let's get out of here." He picked up her parcel.

"Just don't make up for it when you get back," she admonished, as he took her elbow and guided her with courtliness through the passage between the tables, toward the doorway. He opened the door for her. "For you," he offered, as he took her arm, "only a glass of wine at mealtimes."

Out in the street, she pressed his arm under her breast. "Eight meals a day, huh?" she tested, smiling at him.

Ruth had the free-swinging stride of the middle-American woman. As she strode along, with her free hand she swung her pocketbook alongside her. It was a pace that sang of open spaces and horizons that never ended. Her hair, as she paced along, bobbed from side to side, like Nebraskan wheat, thought Conan, and as always when he walked with her, he made a conscious effort not to compare her presence to the mousy cling of many European women.

Conan, with no more recognition than Ruth, held up a hand in dubious greeting to an individual resembling a painter, who rushed past them in the street declaiming to himself in a loud voice. He carried two large cans of paint and threw, almost barked, a laughing word at Conan that sounded like *"amigo!"*

"Friend?" asked Ruth.

"I'm not sure. . . . I may have met him in one of the bars."

Silently then, they reached the front door of Conan's apartment house. They neither of them saw a pile of black plastic garbage bags on the sidewalk outside the door, nor did they hear the roaring and grinding of the trucks on Seventh Avenue; they were both only aware that soon they would be again in each other's arms, and that she had already forgiven him, even though she did not quite perfectly understand yet why he was going away from her. He was her man, she was his woman, that they both knew, and that, for the time being, was enough for them.

Later, much later, in the quiet dark, Ruth said sleepily, "If you sail a boat like you sail a woman, Conan, you're gonna win that stupid race."

"Hmmm?" he murmured. "Making up for lost time. . . ."

"What do you do alone at sea?" she asked drowsily, as she gently caressed him.

"Wha—?"

"Whaddaya do at sea all on your own for months at a time?"

"Tie a knot in it," Conan replied. They both slept then, locked together, with the pain of the coming parting held at quiet bay.

Chapter 2

FROM THE PLANE, as it descended to land, central Lisbon looked as quaint and colorful as Ruth's dreams and Conan's remembrances of it—a central valley of crowded, narrow streets and spacious plazas surrounded by seven hills built over with ancient pastel-painted dwellings, most of them topped with rust colored tiles, and one of the hills crowned by the child's picture-book castle of San Jorge, its brave flags whipped by the breeze atop its biscuit-hued ramparts.

The TAP airliner had departed from New York crowded, except for Ruth and Conan, with Portuguese-Americans heading for the old country. They mostly spoke English in the broad vowels of New England. Somewhere over mid-Atlantic a transformation had come over them. After dinner had been served, they—the men, mostly—started to move around the aisles, greeting each other, and as groups catalyzed and dissolved and others formed, so the language changed from English to Portuguese, so the gestures intensified, the smiles broadened, and the laughter rang, and the men, most of them past middle age, seemed younger, and sturdier, and stronger, and less anxious and careworn.

"It's a sea change," Conan had observed.

Conan had thought better than to cable ahead to book a hotel. "If we stay at one of those American-operated chain hotels, we might just as well be in Denver or Chicago, and everything will cost at least a third

[13]

more," he had explained. Instead, they had been driven at breakneck speed to the main square of Lisbon, the Rossio. Then, after the ancient green taxi took yet another sharp corner on what seemed to Ruth to be two wheels, they halted in yet another broad square, less crowded than the Rossio. Ruth got the impression that except for a few buses and a fountain in the middle, the square was deserted and empty.

"Praca de Figueras, Pension Coimbra-Madrid, senhor," cried the rotund cab driver, a red-faced man of fifty or so, who had sung out of tune, ostensibly to himself, most of the way from the airport.

"Muito bom," enunciated Conan, exhausting two of his dozen words in Portuguese. Ruth looked at him, surprise on her face. Conan explained quietly, "I don't know it; I use French or Spanish here."

With the cab driver's help, they carried their luggage up three flights of wide, dingy stairs crowded with men and women, most with fistfuls of paper money, who sat on the steps or leaned against the peeling walls of the stairway. They all chatted away in subdued tones and stared at Ruth and Conan as they passed.

"Wow, I can just imagine that in New York," murmured Ruth.

"They're lottery vendors. This is their sort of office," Conan said, puffing slightly.

"There must be a few thousand bucks among them," observed Ruth as they arrived at the ornate, iron-grilled main door of the pension. The cab driver tugged the bell cord.

"More like a million at a guess," declared Conan.

Inside the door the pension was clean, bright, and well-furnished in the graceful Portuguese way, stark and pure and well-proportioned. The pension owner's eldest son, on desk duty, immediately recognized Conan from his previous stay five years before. He stared for a second at Conan, gasped, and ran into the family living room to return to the desk followed by his whole family—father, mother, grandfather, six brothers, three sisters, an aunt, and a male cousin on a visit from Oporto, as he rapidly explained in a mixture of Portuguese, Spanish, broken French, and fractured English.

"She con here, Senhor Conan, fron Oporto, on faire le plus bueno vino alli, Engleez likee ver mucho, no?" Eldest son turned from Conan to Ruth, whom all the girls and women were inspecting minutely, from the top of her head to her toes, shod in gray suede boots. "La senhora es Engleeze tambien?"

Everyone in the crowded office, except for two small girls who shyly smiled, stared seriously at Ruth.

"No—Americana," explained Conan, grinning at Ruth's embarrassment. Everyone broke into wide smiles.

"Ah, América, ver bueno, muitos Portuguesas alli. . . ." There was a general applause of approving murmurs from all the assembled family.

"Con zees way, I har very bueno room—only ten dollar . . ." Eldest Son invited them, as he gently made way through the throng.

Their room, long, wide, high, airy, and bright, overlooked the Praca de Figueras, across to the steep, villa-covered hill a mile away, on top of which, like a castellated pie crust atop a heaped fruit salad, lay the long walls of the fortress of San Jorge. Ruth quickly glanced around the room and took in the large dark-wooded bedstead with its quilted covers, the small desk, the ebonylike chest of drawers, the two chairs, and the curtain of the shower stall. Lightly, she moved across to one of the windows and leaned out. Below, the townsfolk, having finished their siesta, milled about on their business, much of which, in Lisbon, is carried out on the street. Above, the fat cumulus clouds, fresh from the ocean, scurried across the breezy March sky toward the castle ramparts in the distance.

"Noisy," Ruth called to Conan over her shoulder, "but the view is . . . magnifico!"

Conan joined her at the window. He reached out past her to both sides, took hold of the two massive window shutters which were swung back against the outside wall, and closed them. "I wrote half a book in this room," he confided, as if to himself, "there." He turned, in the now silent room, reached for Ruth, and urgently kissed her on the lips.

An hour and a century later she lazily murmured to him, "I still think you're crazy, Conan." Her voice was small and low and she spoke as if in her sleep.

Conan reached over to her and gently fondled her breast. She did not stir. He lightly stroked the sweeping line below her breast to her thigh. Still she did not stir. He let his hand rest delicately on the mound of her belly. Lying thus, Conan shut the thoughts of the coming meetings, the hard effort, the struggles, and the possible triumph ahead, out of his consciousness. "Houghton's not due here until Sunday, and the race doesn't start until Thursday. Let's try to forget it, Ruth; we've two nights together here before the thing starts. Let's just make the most of it, hmm?"

Ruth showed no sign that she had heard what he had murmured. Conan, as he dozed off, felt glad, although he could not fathom why.

When they rose and readied and left the pension, dusk was falling.

"It's like some kind of surrealistic vision," exclaimed Ruth, as they emerged from the street door onto the crowded sidewalk. "To be surrounded by all these people in modern clothes . . . well, most of them . . ." Her eyes followed four gypsy women with nut brown faces, dressed in long skirts of bright, clashing colors, with bright, flashing eyes, who talked loudly and laughed as they lithely sidled past. ". . . and all the traffic honking, and then to look up there,"—she raised her chin in the direction of the castled hill—"it's something out of this world . . . like Disneyland . . . only it's real."

The long castle walls glowed amber in the last rays of the sun dying in the western sky. All around and below the glowing walls, the houses, seemingly piled on top of one another in their thousands, reflected the light in azure, lavender, rose, salmon, lemon, and apricot blazes and the blood-red roofs appeared to pulsate and breathe in the warmth of the evening, as if they were bursting with the emotions they held under them.

"It's the most beautiful city in Europe," claimed Conan, "at least to me. Sure, Paris and Venice are all very well, but there's all that damned Parisian arrogance and those smelly canals. . . ." They turned the corner, wended their way along a short, crowded street, and emerged into the great Rossio square. "Here the air is fresh and the natives are friendly and . . ." Conan gazed up at the gold-edged clouds passing overhead "the ocean breezes blow right in over the city." Ruth could taste the iodine in the breeze.

Aka's dolphin tribe was now passing through the waters where Kweela's calf, Om, had been conceived two years before. Kweela felt pleasure. She knew the place by the set of the sea, the look of the clouds, and the stars. In her mind the memory-vision of that time was as clear as if it had happened only moments ago. Aka, the scarred leader of the tribe, had made his intentions quite clear. He had signalled to her—1,200 clicks in that one second—and although she had not yet seen him on that day, two years ago, she had received the hologram he had sent to her . . . of the two rocky exposed peaks of the undersea mountain, and the warm waters swirling about the fish-abounding shallows . . . far away in the south, where the tribal females gave birth. The vision-image had focused on a shallow inlet in the rocky islets safe from the threat of the stupid but vicious sharks, and the most terrifying of all—Man, who did not seem to kill because he was hungry, but merely because he wanted to. Huk, the dreamer, one of Aka's male companions, had even signalled that Man did not eat, but Aka had refuted those ideas, and so had Kweela.

Now, Kweela's school of mothers with their offspring, all together, rose to the surface to breathe through their blowholes. Some of the thirty-four mothers pushed their calves up ahead of them with one flipper. As they ascended, the school "agreed" to leap. Up to the sea surface they went, each of the mothers eight to twelve feet long, sleek, gleaming, blue, black, white, and powerful. In a hundred watery eruptions and explosions, fountains of spray shone in the sun, green, orange, blue, and silver. The mothers and calves, together, within a split second of each other, broke the surface and leapt and rolled and somersaulted in the air, eight, ten, twelve feet. One mother, Kweela's close friend Sheena, shot into the sky higher than all the others—sixteen feet—and as she did so she twisted herself over and over five times. Then, as they all crashed back into the sea, their speed and weight sent great sheets of sparkling white spray in all directions. As they fell, their quick eyes enjoyed the rainbow colors as the sunshine caught the spray and mist, and they revelled in the delighted grunts, clicks, and squeals of the youngsters as they leapfrogged each other, crisscross, and tumbled back into the sea. Below again, all was cool and calm and blue. Although there were 142 signal groups, each of four separate transmissions, coming at her from the 142 other dolphins in the tribe, Kweela, with Om close to her side, could sense no urgency in them, no alarms. Down into the depths they all went, Om almost touching Kweela's sensitive skin, at a rush. Their tails pushed up and down, up and down, 120 strokes a minute, until at 250 feet depth they levelled out and slowed down, all still grouped together, ready to rise again to the surface of the sea, all revelling in life and their dreams.

As he and Ruth crossed the wide Rossio, Conan thought of the first time he had visited Lisbon. The memory was dimming, but he knew it must have been in late 1941. He had been an able seaman at the time, one of a hastily gathered mob of semiamateurs gotten together somehow by the Admiralty to commission an ancient three-funnelled cruiser, which some genius in Whitehall had imagined would be fit consort for a convoy out to Malta past the iron Axis gauntlet of U-boats and dive-bombers. The ship had been forced to call at Lisbon for repairs.

Of the fifteen merchant ships that left England, only two had gotten through to Malta. They themselves, in the three-funnelled wonder, had received Kesselring's coup de grace, in a welter of flying iron and burning fuel oil, only a hundred miles short of the beleaguered island. Conan thought better than to talk to Ruth of the sea and the hazards of the sea, so he pointed out to her the Pastilleria Suisse, an outside pavement cafe.

"That was the espionage stamping grounds of Europe in the war," he told Ruth. There was no need to explain to her which war. The other conflicts he had been engaged in, Greece, Cyprus, Malaya, Korea, he referred to as "fracases" or "affairs."

For fun, they sat at a table at the north end of the parade of tables,

which had been the Axis end of the promenade, and Ruth giggled while
Conan, his eyes sparkling, in an impossibly thick German accent, made
up hilarious signals about casual passersby "to be sent back to Abwehr
headquarters in Berlin."

Then Conan was silent. Now and then he looked briefly at the sky
and the passing clouds overhead. Ruth knew that he was anticipating
the race, longing to go down to the waterfront, to the yacht *Josephine*,
to look over its lines, to touch it and fondle it and take command of the
thing—a collection of nuts and bolts and bits of wire. In brief glances
she watched him and wondered how long he could stand to be away
from the boat. In a moment of pain she was filled with a sense of im-
pending loss, but she determined not to spoil this perfect day. Conan
looked at her and smiled and they rose to cross the square, still in
silence.

Ahead of them, across the wide Rossio, beyond the Dom Enrique col-
umn, another hill, adorned with villas and mansions and palaces and
alive with gardens and bursts of flowers, rose steeply up to golden shafts
of sunlight shining on the bases of the clouds. As they crossed the
square, startled flights of pigeons wheeled and swooped around them.
They stood for a few minutes by the statue and drank in the scene all
around them. There were hawkers, little old men dressed in black, who
lugged huge straw baskets heaped with oranges and green peas and cab-
bages. Women, some young, some middle-aged, with bare feet and
strong limbs and gold chains around their necks, balanced wooden trays
of fish on their heads as they passed gracefully across the plaza. Sitting
on the base of the statue and standing around on the mosaic-patterned
paving, a dozen lottery ticket sellers displayed hundreds of *bilhetes* which
fluttered and flapped on rickety wooden frames like blackboard easels.
All around the square, on the sidewalks, dozens more hucksters had set
up their wooden trays crammed with cheap notions, while others
strolled around, their necks festooned with a score and more of gaudy
ties, or with a dozen shining, lumpy wristwatches on each arm.

Arm in arm, silently trying to take in the seemingly chaotic scenes
around them, Ruth and Conan passed by the central station, "which
looks like an opera house," she observed, and the opera house, "ought
to be a station," he rejoined, and led her onto the wide, noisy Avenida
da Liberdade, a parade of *fin de siècle* buildings, grassy parkways, pavement cafes, and gaudy umbrellas. Even here, on the Champs Elysées of
Lisbon, multicolored lines of washed clothing, baskets of flowers, and
birdcages decorated the upper stories of some of the buildings. All along
the sidewalk, groups of people, some all male, some mixed, old and

young, moved slowly, hesitantly, and stopped frequently while one of their number gesticulated and stressed a point in the debate to the gathering, laughing or serious.

"It's a bit like being in a stage show . . . you know, like the scene at Ascot in *My Fair Lady*," Ruth exclaimed. "Everyone is inspecting everyone else, the way they stare—"

"No harm in it; it's the custom," explained Conan. "They expect you to stare back. It's all hands in, here; a sort of togetherness, as you say. The men consider that they're paying you a compliment and the women . . . well, I suppose they're warning you off."

All the tables near the serving booth were crowded. They eventually found one a hundred yards away from it, and from there watched the passing scene for twenty minutes.

"Life is slower here than in New York," observed Ruth, just as a waiter arrived at their table. He was a white-haired little man of about sixty-five. About him was an air of sad courtesy. He wore heavy glasses and a white apron down to the ankles of his boots, which were shiny and new and squeaked as he moved.

Conan ordered ginger beer for Ruth ("You must try it. Lisbon is the only place on the Continent where they make real ginger beer") and coffee and Drambuie for himself as Ruth grinned and shook her head slightly.

"Sim, senhor," acknowledged the waiter. He bobbed his ancient head and creaked off. Five minutes later he was back with a paper tablecloth and two napkins, which he silently laid on the table and weighted down with an ashtray. He then creaked off again, the hundred yards back to the booth. Another five minutes passed and again the waiter appeared at their table. "Would the senhora and senhor care for a snack . . . ? We have mussels and clams and prawns in cream sauce and ham rolls and steak sandwich . . ."

Conan ordered two small steak sandwiches to tide them over until dinner.

"Sim, senhor." The waiter creaked off another hundred yards, to return in five minutes with knives and forks, which he gravely laid on the table. On his next passage to the booth and back he bore the drinks. They waited another ten minutes for him to return with the food. By the time Conan paid the check—all of three dollars—the waiter had creaked and squeaked to the booth five times.

"That makes roughly a thousand yards," estimated Conan. "And they grossed three dollars, and the waiter practically kissed my hand for the fifty-cent tip," he observed to a vastly amused Ruth.

They crossed the road again and made their way through the throng on the sidewalk up the slight incline of the Avenida. They passed a dozen women dressed in black with armsful of straw hats and a score of men with hands full of dark glasses, and they stopped and watched four laborers crouched on the roadside. The men tapped at large gray stones, which they deftly split into tiny cubes. These they methodically, patiently, set in intricate patterns in the newly cemented area of the sidewalk. Then they watched as other men, with wooden pestles as tall as themselves, pounded the stones with rhythmic swings until they were firmly imbedded in the cement, evenly and good for another hundred years.

They waited with a small crowd at the bottom of a steep incline which gives out onto the Avenida. Conan passed a coin to a legless beggar who rushed himself along on a tiny cart.

Ruth peered up the narrow alleyway which faded away up in dim light. She read aloud the street sign, as a question. "Calcada de Gloria?— Something to Glory?"

"Rise of Glory," translated Conan.

"What a lovely name for such a crummy street."

"Wait—this is really something, Ruth."

Even as Conan spoke a dark shape made its quiet way down the hill toward them in the twilight, at first black, then gray, it finally revealed itself as a trolley car—but the most oddly shaped trolley car Ruth had ever seen. The downhill end of the heavily scrolled Edwardian passenger compartment was a good six feet above the street level, perched on a spindly iron chassis which conformed to the steepness of the hill at an angle of thirty degrees, while the uphill end of the passenger compartment almost scraped the ground. It reminded Ruth of some kind of insect she had once surprised in a hotel bathtub in Bermuda.

They silently pushed their way on board the trolley among a jostling crowd which included three women with baskets of flowers and one with a cage of four live hens. Ruth made to sit, but Conan firmly led her to the downhill end of the cabin to stand at the window. "Don't miss this," he said as, with a jerk, the trolley started to move silently up the hill.

After a few moments, when she could see over the roofs of the near building, the city, strings, necklaces, and diadems of twinkling lights below seemed to drop away from them as the car rose up the incline, and then, like a theatrical backdrop, the Castle of San Jorge, its ramparts and towers flooded with golden light, hove into view, leaving Ruth, for a few moments, speechless with wonder. Even Conan, although he had seen it a dozen times, was still moved by the drama of the scene.

As the trolley reached the top of the mile-long hill with a slight bump, Conan grabbed Ruth's arm to steady her. "How's that?" he asked with a grin. "Welcome to the Bairro Alto!"

"Makes the view of Manhattan look ... mundane," she declared as they alighted.

"Only two other views like it," he said. "Rio de Janeiro at dawn, from the ocean ..." They heard the sound of plaintive music coming from a small tavern. They started across the road, heading toward it.

"And the other?"

"Princess Street, Edinburgh, on a cold winter's night when a mist lies near the ground in the valley below the castle."

Ruth laughed, low, and grabbed Conan's arm. "What a contrast," she exclaimed, "Rio and Edinburgh! What would Freud make of that?"

"Coffee and Drambuie."

She shook her head, smiling the while, as they passed a handsome youth idling in front of an iron-grilled window. Inside the window but in front of a curtain, in the shadow, a young woman sat. Both were gazing at each other in absolute silence.

"Courting," explained Conan laconically.

Ruth was taken aback, almost unable to believe what she had seen. "I thought that went out with crinolines," she exclaimed quietly.

"In Portugal, nothing that's worthwhile goes out," he replied, "and sometimes silence is worthwhile."

Before Ruth had time to take him up on the matter, they reached the door of the tavern, which was piled around with green plant fronds.

Inside the tavern half the tables were unoccupied. At first Ruth wondered if they should stay, but Conan reassured her that they were early. The headwaiter led them to a table inside an alcove let into the plain whitewashed walls. On the opposite side of the tavern, behind an ornate mahogany bar, varnished hogsheads of wine were stacked, four rows of them, all the way up to the great rafters of the wooden ceiling, from which hung hams and sides of bacon, as well as wire flower baskets brilliant with blooms.

The other customers in the tavern were mainly either family groups or couples, most of them, Ruth felt instinctively, very accustomed to each others' company. Ruth let Conan order for her. A *vichyssoise*, a delicious light white wine, *bacalhau*—cod cooked as only the Portuguese can cook it—and a *Serra*—goat cheese. For the finale Conan chose finely sugared oranges *à la maltaise*. They had just started to eat the dessert when suddenly the lights in the tavern all dimmed and a hush descended. Even the noise from the kitchen ceased. In the gloom Ruth could see that the tavern was now crowded, at almost full capacity. The waiters stopped serving and stood against the walls, their silver trays held down in front of them. A noisy German tourist at one of the tables was hissed into silence. A spotlight lit up one of the tables, which was adorned simply with a white cloth, the same as all the other tables. At it sat two men, one middle-aged, the other young. The older man strummed a Portuguese guitar, which reminded Ruth of an oversized banjo, but had a more fluid, delicate tone. He carried the melody. The younger man filled in the chords, heavy and plaintive, on a Spanish guitar.

A woman emerged out of the shadows behind the musicians. She was dressed all in black, with a black shawl thrown around her shoulders. She was not young, nor was she beautiful, yet when she leaned her head back and closed her eyes, trancelike, and surrendered to the sadness of pain and parting, there was something, it seemed to Conan, very beautiful in her acceptance of fate.

As the music of the *fado* rose and fell, slowed and quickened, it became a wild cry of pain, of parting, of jealousy, of loss and ashes and fire and guilt and despair and longing and hopeless desolation. It was a moan from the depth of the singer's soul and into it she heaped and she shovelled all her past tribulations and cast them at everyone sitting in the tavern. Ruth, after one song, almost overcome by the anguish of the *fado* music, begged Conan to take her out.

They moved out through the silent, serious crowd at the door and crossed the road again to the small, dark tree-overhung park atop the cliff that overlooks the city center. There they stood, side by side, for half an hour or more, and gazed at the carpet of twinkling diamonds a thousand feet below them, from the pulsing loom of Campo Grande in the north, down past the magic glow of the Castle of San Jorge, past the leave-taking lamps of Lisbon docks and beyond, to an ocean steamer, her lights all ablaze as she moved slowly out into the blackness of the Tagus River.

Trying to hold back the tears she felt, Ruth clung to Conan's arm as she watched the steamer pass out of sight toward the ocean. She thought of his coming departure. She looked at his face. He, too, was gazing toward the darkened river. He turned and looked into her eyes, calm and unsmiling. She reached up and brought his mouth down to hers and kissed him and pressed her body close to him. She kissed him passionately and long and after the first bittersweet taste of her kiss, as she tightened his hold around her, Conan knew again the stir at his loins. She sensed it and pressed herself to him. He thought of the time long ago when he had been a jaunty young sailor and had imagined that by the time he reached fifty all this would be but a memory. Now, he thought, as Ruth eased herself away from him, it was even worse—better?—worse?—it certainly was deeper. So deep inside him, the insatiable longing, the wanting of her, as to cause him physical pain. He held her away from him and looked at her. There were tears in her eyes, yet she was smiling for him.

"Come on, Ruth." He took her elbow gently. "Let's go and have a nightcap," he said, as he led her away from the railings, out of the little park, back toward the cockeyed trolley and the Rise of Glory.

Chapter 3

NEXT MORNING, Saturday, they set out to visit the Castle of San Jorge. The day was sunny and fine, an early spring day in Lisbon. Conan wore the same corduroys he had worn in New York—he would wear them ashore until they dropped off him, Ruth thought with amusement. It was strange, for a man so impetuous, so ready to pick up stakes and voyage the world at the drop of a hat, how he was also a man of certain idiosyncrasies, how he wore the same clothes and used the same restaurant, the same bar (when he wasn't writing), until they almost seemed to be a part of him, and he of them. When they had gone to the Pastilleria Suisse for breakfast that morning, Conan had insisted that they wait a few minutes. Gruffly, he had made the excuse of buying a newspaper across the square, until the table they had occupied the previous evening was vacant; they had even sat on the same chairs.

Ruth wore a white peasant blouse and a flowered cotton skirt, with white shoes she had hurriedly picked up at Macy's in New York on their way to the airport as Conan sat impatiently in a cab outside. Now, as they strolled arm in arm down the Rua Agosta toward Black Horse Square, Conan told her of how Lisbon was reputed to have been founded by Ulysses and he spoke of kings and queens—Don Afonso, Queen Leonora, King Manuel—and explained to her as they passed ancient churches and palaces who built what. Ruth, half-listening to him, reflected that the panic over the shoes had been completely unnecessary. Here, there were shoe shops galore, their windows proud with elegant creations at only half the prices of New York.

They came to a narrow street, as straight as a die and as long as a rifle shot—"Rua dos Bacalhoeiros" Ruth read the sign aloud.

"Cod-Fisherman's Street," explained Conan. They stared at the House of Pointed Stones, its facade covered with strange, pointed granite blocks facing outward. The play of sun and shadow on the sharp angles was a triumph of natural decoration. It reminded Ruth of a rhinoceros or an armadillo. They visited the *Se*, the Cathedral, the oldest church in Lisbon, with its rose windows half as big as a basketball court "Built in 1147," Conan read from a guide pamphlet. Ruth calculated quickly. "Well, let's see, 1147 from 1981 . . . that's 834 years."

Ruth tied a gauze scarf loosely over her head and they, both feeling awed, walked slowly through the chancel, a silent treasury of intricately worked plaster and marble and on through the ambulatory, a vast, domed hall from which radiated chapels in which sunlight streamed through the stained glass of centuries-old windows. Solid-seeming oblique shafts of blue and gold and scarlet and silver pierced the still gloom and shone on the tombs of kings and saints and knights and martyrs, and played on the carved emblematic shields of love and respect and remembrance. "And fear, too," observed Conan, as their muted footsteps echoed into the cloister, where a magnificent Romanesque grill of black iron curleycues—thousands of them—and draped behind it a great blood red curtain, almost a thousand feet square, guarded what they guarded from prying eyes.

Out in the spring sunshine again, a sultry wind blew. They strolled slowly under newly blossoming trees, still arm in arm, up the hill past the little platform-park of Santa Luzia and the imposing silhouette of the church of Saint Vincent-outside-the-walls. Conan pointed out to Ruth the crumbled remains of the twelve-hundred-year-old Moorish city wall. They sat for a while on the stones and Conan brought to life for her visions of splendor and love and terror and triumph as she, turning one of the small stones over and over in her hands, listened to him recount some of the history of the wall.

They wandered, almost nonchalantly, by an old house which leaned drunkenly against the Moorish wall. They found it was a museum of decorative arts. They entered. It was a mansion full of rooms from all the ages back to the twelfth century, and actually seemed to be still inhabited. All the rooms were crammed full of precious artifacts—furniture, gold, and silver tablewear, richly shot brocades, carpets, clocks, chandeliers, paintings, carvings and statuettes, suits of armor (there was even one "tailored" for a child of six!), painted ceilings, ornate gilt-framed mirrors, spinning wheels, strange-looking kitchen utensils, and heart-wrenching little paint boxes and combs and ladies' looking glasses used long, long ago for vanity which has gone the way of all vanity, except for that which, in the height of its beauty, had been depicted in the dark portraits on the walls. The bequest of the artist only is not vanity.

They passed two urchins, shaven-headed, elf-faced, and barefoot, of about six years old who were sitting on a house doorstep. They were eating with their fingers from tin cans. Ruth smiled at them.

"*E servido, senhora,*" they both greeted her in piping voices.

Conan grinned.

"What did they say?" she asked him.

"*It is served.* They meant the food, of course. They're offering to share it with you. It's the common thing here."

She turned and smiled at the two boys. They shaded their eyes with sticky hands from the sun's glare and grinned at her. Both had their front teeth missing. For a moment she hesitated, then called to them, "*Bom dia!*"

Both lads saluted, fingers to foreheads. "*Bom dia, senhor e senhora! Que vais com Dios!*"

Ruth turned and bent her head. "Well, well," she said softly. "Where've I been this past ten years!"

They passed through the archway of the main entrance to the Castle of San Jorge, "There to commune with the ghosts of randy Romans, vicious Visigoths, and sensuous Saracens," he told her, as they made their way over the rough cobbled street and onto a gravel walk between lush grass lawns, which covered most of the area of the castle grounds.

Ruth stopped and gasped in astonishment as soon as they had covered the rise just inside the castle. Typically, Conan watched her face as, at first in wonder, then in delight, she gaped at the stupendous view.

Twenty yards in front of her, down a gentle slope, a low, biscuit-colored wall, only three feet high but ten feet thick, contained the acres of grassy forecourt on the rise of which she stood. At intervals along the wall, olive trees, gnarled and twisted with age, their green oily leaves glistening, gave shade. Between the trees a score of great bronze cannons mutely, quaintly now, glowered over miles and miles of tiled roofs and steeples and church towers, gables and mansards, chimneys and windows, streets, avenues, and facades which stretched out below the castle into the distance, all crowded, hemmed in between the house-covered heights of the six other hills of Lisbon on three sides, and on the other side the azure blue Tagus River.

Conan pointed out to her the Salazar Bridge, which reminded Ruth of the Golden Gate and which led over the bluffs on the south bank of the Tagus, past the immense monument of Christ, seven hundred feet high. His arms were, she could see, outstretched in white benefaction under a sky blue and clear and ocean clean.

"Belém's over there, beyond the bridge, on this side of the river," Conan told her, pointing it out. "That's where the boat is," he said. *From whence blew the wind*, he thought. *Southwest, six knots, the way those olive tree leaves twinkle and shiver. The wind should veer around to the northwest by Thursday, with any luck. Just the job for getting the hell south down past Cape Saint Vincent . . .*

She looked at his face. He was staring intently, eyes almost closed into slits, at a point just somewhere near the city end of the bridge. Suddenly he turned and caught her look, and wished he had not yet mentioned the boat. He took her arm and led her down to the wall, where they sat for an hour looking at the houses and gardens and trees and flowered walks far below them, all laid out like a child's toy town, but Ruth was sadly aware every time Conan's eyes strayed to a sail on the river, or back to the spot by the bridge. She knew it was unreasonable to feel this way. She wondered to herself if it was jealousy she felt whenever she thought of *Josephine*, or whether it was merely the knowledge that the boat was the instrument of his leaving her for the bleak months ahead.

She determined not to let him know how she felt about their parting. It was strange. She was caught between two stools. If she ranted and raved and cried and threatened she would be playing the role of the scorned woman. If she suffered in silence she would be playing the (to her) ridiculous role of the loyal little woman. She made up her mind to play herself, to put love to one side, no matter how much she loved him. She would be herself. She had her work, she had her friends, she would live her own life until he returned. What they'd had between them had been good—very, very good, the best she would ever have.

Nothing would or could, she was sure, ever change that. She looked at Conan again. Strange, she thought, how he shed his age at times— when he was with her—in bed especially. He had told her it was because he'd been at sea most of his life, and while that aged a man's head beyond the ken of landsmen, it preserved his body. He had told her it was because of all the activity, all the isolation, all the peace of mind, all the comparative freedom from outside pressures and commercial stress.

She smiled to herself as she remembered the time they had discussed a cigarette advertisement that had featured a rugged-faced cowboy. She had admired the craggy-visaged model. "Symbol of freedom?" he had scoffed. "Cowboys? Christ, the ocean sailors make them look like office runners! Free? Those saddle pounders, compared to small-craft ocean roamers, are about as free as bus drivers!" True, he had been a little drunk at the time, but she had to admit there was probably something in what he said; the man in the ad looked a little *too* handsome . . . a mite *too* rugged.

Nothing could ever change what had passed between them. For her it had been the happiest period in her life. His gruff bluntness, his down to earth disdain of pretensions and shallowness had, at first, put her off, but to her he had always been honest. He had never, as her ex-husband and her previous lovers had done, put her anywhere near a pedestal. He treated her as a dear friend, as an equal being on the face of the earth, whose hand and heart and mind and body he loved and whose passage, alone, through the maze of experience called life, he eased and made more gentle. Colors were more brilliant when he was near her. Besides, she told herself, if anyone could make her laugh, Conan could.

Suddenly, from a small arched doorway in the castle keep, six all-white peacocks strutted out, like little ships in line ahead. Both Ruth and Conan watched them, bemused, as one by one they spread out their tails into magnificent ivory fans dotted with blue and red commas. Slowly, they strolled over toward the birds.

"Engleez?" a high voice said. He was small and skinny. At first Conan thought it was a boy. He turned and saw that it was a little old man. He had a red face, slightly pockmarked, and a three-day growth of white whiskers which framed, like snow in a roof gutter, his long face. He wore a shiny blue frock coat which was too big for him and gray trousers too short for him, and on his chest dangled a brass medallion about four inches across. "I am zhe keeper of zhe birds," he explained. A clock nearby struck eleven.

Conan grinned at him and nodded. "Yes, English," he said. No sense in complicating matters, he thought.

"Ah, Engleez. Many Engleez pippel con here," said the old man, smiling at Ruth.

"What beautiful peacocks," she exclaimed. "Do you breed them?"

"Ah yes, I brid zhem," the keeper replied.

"I don't think I've ever seen white peacocks before," she said. "Why are they white?"

"You see, senhora," the old man smiled, "we do not have any snow in Lisbon, and zhe cheeldren do not know what zhe snow look like, so we brid zhe birds to look like zhe snow."

Conan laughed and slapped his hand on his pocket. He took Ruth's arm.

"Come on, time for lunch," he said. "Good-bye, senhor." He shook the little old man's hand and they moved away. Ruth still stared at the birds.

"What a lovely story," she said, laughing softly.

"Yes," said Conan, "I'll bet he tells it to all the girls," he said and laughed again, "but bless him all the same. It's a good line."

They walked back down the hilly streets to the Cais de Sodre, the tenderloin district near the docks. It is a district of narrow streets lined with flower- and birdcage-bedecked bars, cafes, restaurants, ship chandler's and sailor's clothing stores with windows full of canvas and cotton, blazes of blue and red. Unbelievable sunburned nautical characters of all ages, who, to Ruth, looked as if they had just stepped out of a stage show of *Treasure Island*, wandered, clothed in red-and-white and blue-and-white striped shirts, wide-sleeved smocks and white bell-bottomed pants, bandanas around their heads, some barefoot, in and out of the bars, or played dice for drinks inside the shady doorways.

Conan, as they ate a plain, cheap meal, *caldo verde* of sausage, potatoes, and cabbage with seafood and good rose wine, all for three dollars, remembered that the Arizona and Texas bars, each with a hundred or so girls, had been, years before, in this same street. Perhaps they were still there. He didn't need them now as he had then, he thought gratefully, as he discussed with Ruth how she would handle the subletting of his apartment.

"Someone steady, not someone who's promiscuous, or likely to just take off into the blue," he said.

"Someone like you," she rejoined, smiling at him.

"Yes," he said seriously, as he signed a power of attorney for her.

"At approximately five cents, this must be one of the great travel bargains of Europe," said Conan, as he and Ruth boarded the train at Cais de Sodre station, bound five miles along the shoreline for Belém. The train was crowded. They stood, clinging to roof-straps. All around them peasants, sailors, and factory workers talked loudly and merrily.

The first couple of miles was mainly vistas of slums—yet still colorful—and dreary factory walls bedaubed with Communist slogans. "Relics of the gentle revolution of 1974," explained Conan. "It was all very sedate—the soldiers stuck flowers in their rifles. God knows, after thirty-odd years of Salazar's dictatorship, they deserved a bit of a binge."

"I can't imagine communism attracting these people," said Ruth, looking around the crowded open train carriage. "They seem to be far too individualistic."

"That's why it never took," Conan explained. "Look." He ducked his head and pointed his beard at a wall mural. It was a huge painting, al-

most a hundred yards long, executed in the "socialist reality" tech-
nique—dozens of "heroic" workers, men and women, all striding
toward the Marxist Utopia, which evidently was somewhere on the vacant lot between the railroad line and the factory wall.

"Dramatic," she said.

"I've seen them all over the world, from Mexico to Lithuania," said
Conan. "But there's a difference here . . . see, all the faces are distinctly
different from one another. What they depict here is not a mass of people, but a group of individuals . . . any one of whom looks as if he's about
to take off on his own road any minute."

As the train stopped, a working man in light blue coveralls offered
Ruth her seat. No sooner had she sat down than a chubby old lady on
the seat opposite her, dressed all in black, offered Ruth an apple almost
as red and shiny as her own cheeks. Ruth, embarrassed and a little con-
fused, shook her head, smiling. The old lady then, wordlessly, reached
up and offered the apple to Conan, who, with a wide smile and cour-
teous "*Obrigado, senhora,*" accepted it, rubbed it on the sleeve of his corduroy jacket, and bit into it, winking at Ruth as he did so. The old lady,
seeing him wink, laughed softly. When they alighted at Belém, minutes
later, Conan, with the half-eaten apple in hand, blew the old lady a kiss.
She replied by rolling her merry blue eyes at him as she threw her head
back and jiggled her basket against the gold crucifix on her black-vested
breasts.

"What a marvelous old dear!" said Conan on the platform.

Ruth jogged his arm. "Watch it, Conan," she murmured jocosely, pre-
tending jealousy. "The old crone probably poisoned it."

In the bright afternoon sunshine they ambled through a tree-lined
park and watched swans swimming under genteel fountains in ornate
pools, fended off a half-dozen incredibly tiny shoeshine boys and tie
hucksters, then made their way to the coach museum. There, under me-
ticulously painted, scrolled plaster ceilings, they wondered at a score of
golden royal coaches, each one different, and at the handiwork of their
precious red-plush and silver interiors. As they stood alone in the vast
hall—they were the only visitors—it was as if they could hear the car-
riages whispering of the scenes of past pomp and glory they had
witnessed.

They inspected, awed by the workmanship displayed, the finest of
pride from past centuries—chaises, litters, berlins, pleasure carts, ca-
lashes, saddles, horse trappings decorated in silver, riding accessories,
boots, spurs, uniforms, livery, court arrays and dress for the royal hunts,
and the sinister armories and trappings of horse warfare.

They passed along the main street of Belém, old houses with colon-naded ground floors cluttered with shops full of chrome chairs and plas-tic-topped tables and Japanese radios, and then, suddenly, as if in a fairy tale, Ruth saw before her eyes a miracle in stone. It was as if the rocks of earth had burst out of the ground in a hymn of praise, a poem in liv-ing stone rising up to heaven.

"The Monastery of Jerónimos," explained Conan. "Sacred to all mar-iners . . . or it ought to be. From here the Portuguese sent out the first of the Renaissance ships of discovery, up to 150 years before your Co-lumbus sailed—Diaz, Da Gama, Magellan—they all sailed out from here."

As she listened to Conan, Ruth stared at the intricately detailed sculp-ture on the great west portal—saints with features so alive, so human, that they seemed to breathe, and a lacework of finely carved granite all around them and over them, all the way up to the roof, where Christ surveyed all calmly, His eyes fixed on the far horizon.

Listening to Conan, Ruth's eyes followed the straw-colored highlights and deep shadows of sun-warmed stone filled with saintly angels, angel-ic saints, mitred bishops, martyred disciples, and a repentant Mary Mag-dalene, who crouched below and stared in wonder at the horizon-searching Virgin.

"It all seems so clean and brand new," she exclaimed.

"Clean air—straight from the ocean," he replied.

"What made them do all this, where does it all come from?"

"They sailed in crazy, frail vessels we wouldn't cross the Hudson in," he murmured. "They knew next to nothing about nutrition or medi-cine, or even what the world looked like and they sailed into the terror of the unknown. They had only their courage and their faith . . ." Conan looked at Ruth. "And that's what all this tries to express . . ." He hes-itated for a moment, thinking. "Guts and God," he finally said. "That's all they had—and in the end it's all that counts, and that's where it came from, I reckon."

And love, Ruth thought, but she remained silent, because perhaps that was what he meant. They were silent for a moment. She knew—under-stood—his mind was on the waiting boat.

"When are we going to see *Josephine?*" she found herself saying.

"What? . . . Oh, she's over there, back through the park," he replied casually, as if it were the last thing on his mind. "But I thought you might want to go inside the monastery. There's a wonderful Renais-sance high chapel . . ."

Ruth slowly turned and looked at him for a few seconds. Conan looked down and kicked a pebble with one foot. "You're a terrible kidder, Conan. You know damn well you don't want to go inside. All you want to do is get to the damned boat." She seized his arm and pulled him, grinning, away from the monastery doorway. "All right," she said, "let's go."

They walked through the waterfront park and across the busy Avenida de Brasilia and soon came within the smell of low-tide seaweed and the sound of the wire rigging from a hundred sailing vessels frapping on metal masts. The three-acre square yacht basin was full of boats tied up stern to the high surrounding jetties. Along the seaward side of the basin were the race boats—Ruth knew they were the race boats. There was, to her, a sinister animal-like crouch to their appearance. Conan's pace quickened as they passed by the line of sleek hulls cluttered with chrome fittings. Conan read the names on the hulls out loud as he strode along. "*Ocean Pacer, Sir John Falstaff, Ocean Viking*—the Swedes are in, eh? *Flagrante Delicto* . . ." He looked around, craning his neck. "No one around at all. They must all be in town. *Etoile du Sud*—I wonder who's sailing her? Surely not Terlain?" Conan's voice suddenly was lower. "Ah, there she is!" He turned to Ruth. "Pretty as a picture, eh?"

Ruth saw a long, low dark blue hull. She glanced at the silver steering wheel and the massive chrome sheet windlasses, and up at the arrogant-looking anodized golden mainmast.

"She's all locked up—I suppose until Houghton gets here in the morning," Conan said. "No sense in going aboard."

"Then let's go back to Lisbon, Conan. My feet are getting tired," said Ruth, and then she wished she hadn't.

"Okay, but I'd like to look over the others." He nodded toward the other race craft. To Ruth they seemed only a jumble of very expensive playthings. "Look, you rest your feet here a minute, I won't be more than a jiffy." He strode off, his attention focused on the other craft along the basin.

Ruth sat on a low bollard and waited for him. She stared down at *Josephine* and hated it as she had never hated any other inanimate object in her life. She hated *Josephine* so much that she could taste the hatred welling up inside her. She glared at the boat and wished with all her heart that it would sink in its moorings right then and there. With a grimace she pulled herself together and decided that she would ignore the boat, walk further away from it, pretend it was not there, waiting to take Conan away from her. She had resented, much of the time, being a woman at all until Conan had come along. Just to know him, the man in him, made it all worthwhile. Anyway, she asked herself, what fool ever promised that love necessarily meant endless happiness? For a moment she wished that she had not meant her love for Conan, that she could have been . . . frivolous about it all; but then she knew that if she had been frivolous it would not have been love. "So the hell with it," she told herself aloud. She was leaving for New York and her work and her friends and her own life in the morning. There was no stopping—no sense in stopping—a man like Conan once he had made up his mind.

Conan caught up with her. Wordlessly he smiled. She, also wordlessly, reached up for him and kissed him hard. Still silent, they made their way back to the railway station, where, as they waited, Conan amused her with fanciful tales about the other skippers, most of whom he had not yet met, and whom he only imagined and brought to life for her hilariously.

The rest of the day and night was for Ruth bliss, passion, and rapture, until the sweet sorrow of their bodies parting at daybreak.

Chapter 4

NEITHER RUTH NOR CONAN were fond of leave-taking at any time. When the time came for their own parting they liked it even less. At breakfast, at their accustomed table in front of the Pastilleria Suisse, in the taxi out to the airport, and during an interminable wait for a plane which was a mere fifteen minutes late, they made small talk, mainly of the arrangements for Conan's New York apartment and the retention of mail. Ruth agreed to forward any letters from publishers or editors to Conan's agent and to keep the rest herself until his return.

"He's got a copy of my will, too," said Conan, doing his best to sound casual about it. "It's only a formality, of course," he said, embarrassed. "There isn't really much in the kitty."

Ruth hugged his arm. She looked into his eyes directly. "Look after yourself, Conan." His love—her love for him was all that mattered.

He looked at her. "Will you come away with me then? I've a book in my head about the Philippines, a sort of Conradian saga, as well as a thing about this voyage, of course. We could go there to live for a couple of years.... It's cool in the mountains.... Since I've loved you ... my love for you makes me love everything and everyone ... more than ... I've never felt like it before." He stammered as he recognized himself in her, as over all the airport loudspeakers ordered passengers to board for New York. Ruth took the small case which Conan handed her. She

[34]

put it down again on the floor, reached up, and kissed him.

"Look after yourself, Conan. Try to win—for both of us," she murmured. She quickly picked up the case and walked through the doorway onto the tarmac. Conan watched her swing her way firmly to the plane steps, watched her climb the steps, and watched her disappear inside the great jet plane without once looking back.

In a way Conan was glad there were not many people about in the airport, it somehow made the parting easier. He glanced at his watch and, slowly, made his way up the wide stairway to the coffee lounge. He would be able to see Ruth's plane take off from there, through the wide windows, and he could wait there for Mike Houghton's plane from London to arrive in two hour's time. He bought the previous Sunday's *London Globe* newspaper on the way to the coffee lounge, found an empty table, sat down, and leafed through the pages. The paper was last week's edition, but there it was on the front page of the sports section—"Globe Round the World Sailing Race—the Lineup." Below the headline were pictures of most of the boats taking part in the race, with brief details of the boat and skipper.

Ruth's plane started to move out across the tarmac to its take-off station. He watched until it snootily cocked its nose up and confidently, nonchalantly, zoomed off out of sight. He felt numb and relieved at the same time. He turned again to the newspaper. There was a rather fuzzy picture of *Josephine*. "Built," he read, "1973 at Struther's, Southampton. Designers Lightman and Reevers, U.S.A., length overall, 44 feet, length waterline, 38 feet, sloop, sail area 980 square feet (working rig). Placed in Round Britain race, 1978." Pretty good, thought Conan. He read on— "Participant in disastrous Fastnet race, 1979. *Josephine,* with Sean Shaughnessy as skipper and four crew, abandoned the race at midstage and arrived safely back in Falmouth. Fifteen crewmen died in the 1979 Fastnet race, 24 yachts were abandoned, and 138 racing sailors"—Conan whistled softly as he read the numbers—"were rescued by search and rescue services from three NATO countries."

There they go again, thought Conan. Trust the press to play up death and disaster. They must have had a ball with hostages languishing all over the place under threats of death. . . . Funny how the Yanks still hadn't learned that some others were not as they . . .

He focused his eyes back onto *Josephine*'s details. "Skipper Shaughnessy, slated for the Globe £50,000 single-handed round-the-world race, lost his life in a car crash outside London last week. He was returning to London airport from an inquiry, held in Portsmouth, into the Fastnet race debacle. Mike Houghton, *Josephine*'s manager, states that Shaughnessy's place is being taken by Bill Conan, though this has not yet been confirmed. Conan, who skippered the 24-foot *Hobson's Choice* in the Observer single-handed transatlantic race of 1976, was involved in a collision with a power boat six miles from the finishing line in Newport, U.S.A., and, although first in his handicap class, was disqualified."

Conan laid the paper down and stared out of the window. He remembered how the power boat had charged into *Hobson's Choice*. One minute he'd been anxiously dressed for arrival, in a clean jersey and blue jeans and best deck shoes, standing at the helm, excitedly anticipating the end of three weeks of rough going, mainly on cold food, and the next minute he'd been floundering around holding on grimly to a capsized, shattered hull.

As Conan stared through the window, his frown changed to a grin. He recalled his first words when the power boat owner, in a frenetic panic, had hove to. Conan had slowly swum over to the power boat. When the crew had dragged him on board, the owner, a Pickwickian little man in an impossibly immaculate white suit, moaned over him, "Gee, feller, I'm really sorry about this ..." At that moment a U.S. Coast Guard launch had arrived close by and was hailing for Conan to be passed on board it. Conan, dripping wet through and deeply angry, had grabbed the boat owner by the shoulder, shaken him like a terrier, and shouted into his face, "You clumsy bastard!" Then, to the consternation of the power boat crew he had jumped back in the sea and swum the few yards over to the Coast Guard launch, whose ratings hauled him on board their vessel boatless, penniless, and hopping mad. Thus his arrival in America.

Conan turned back to the newspaper account. "As Bill Conan has not been active in ocean racing," he read, "nor, according to reports, even in sailing, for the past four years, his chances in the Globe £50,000 round-the-world race are considered by most experts to be slim, although in an event of this nature, of course, anything can happen. Conan, if he joins *Josephine* in Lisbon early this week, will have his work cut out to accustom himself to the boat in time to make a good showing on the first leg down to a point off the coast of Brazil. Conan was renowned as a hard skipper, a first-class driver; it will be interesting to see what the effect of four years of soft shore life in America have had on his performance in the initial stages of the race."

Conan snorted quietly and turned to the form of the other eight entrants in the race.

"*Sir John Falstaff*," he read. "British, sloop, 55 foot length overall ... skipper Lieutenant Commander Joseph Morgan, forty-two, sponsored by major British yacht clubs ... considered the favorite ... *Ocean Pacer*, British, yawl, 53 feet overall ... skipper John Tyler, forty, this will be his third solo circumnavigation, which will set a new record. Tyler is considered the second favorite ... *Southern Star*, Australian, sloop, 53 feet overall, Paddy Hunt, thirty-five, winner of four single-handed ocean races ... *Flagrante Delicto*, New Zealand, ketch, 46 feet overall, skipper Mary Chatterton, twenty-eight, the only woman entrant, her third single-handed ocean race ... *Etoile du Sud*, French, yawl, 48 feet overall, skipper Jaques Duplessis, forty-four, winner three single-handed ocean races ... *Sundance Kid*, U.S.A., a yawl, 48 feet overall, skipper Jack Hanson, twenty-three, sponsored by an international conglomerate. She is the most extensively equipped vessel in the fleet. Hanson, from California, is a surfing and dinghy-racing champion, but apart from his qualifying thousand-mile passage to Lisbon from U.K., he has had no other single-handed ocean experience. However, because of the sophisticated radio weather-report receiving system, and the radio navigational system, both via satellite, Hanson shares the third favorite place with ... *Ocean Viking*, Swedish, yawl, 47 feet overall, skipper Sven Larsen, forty, winner of five single-handed ocean races, shares third favorite place with Jack Hanson. Here, it will be a case of youthful exuberance and modern technology being pitted against seamanship and hard-earned experience."

Conan shook his head as he read the last name on the list. "*Blytskwiska.*" At first he thought it was a printer's error, then he tried to pronounce it a couple of times, moving his lips silently, and finally he gave up and read on. "Poland, yawl, 44 feet overall, skipper Petr Bartusok, thirty-eight, sponsored by the Polish Railway Worker's Sailing Association. This will be Bartusok's second circumnavigation, but apart from the qualifying passage from Gdynia to Lisbon, his first single-handed ocean event ..." Conan waded through the words until he came across a passage that he read twice. "Of the fifteen yachts on the original entry list that left Weymouth for the passage to Lisbon, the starting line, six dropped out before their arrival in Lisbon. This seems to have been due as much to equipment failure as to the bad weather that was encountered in the Bay of Biscay. General Sir Hubert Alwys-Bother ingham, who at seventy-two years of age set out for the race in his 45-foot yawl *Able*, not only lost his mainmast, but also suffered a heart attack. He died shortly after being picked up by a Royal Navy minesweeper when only three hundred miles out. 'Bobby' Gantry, twenty-two, who set out in the 25-foot folkboat *Rolling Stone*, gave up after the first night, and radioed for a rescue helicopter. Gantry now says that he is opening a disco as he feels it is more suitable to his personality. Gantry, former member of a pop group, stated that he found solo sailing 'very boring, being on my own and going up and down and all that.' "

Conan grinned wryly. The reporter, himself probably bored stiff in the Fleet Street office, must have enjoyed writing that, he thought.

At one o'clock the BOAC plane from London landed. As the line of passengers traipsed across the tarmac Conan caught sight of Mike Houghton bringing up the rear, behind early vacationers and prosperous-looking wine merchants and their families. Conan studied Mike as he approached the wide open entry doors. He was as jaunty as ever, though he was slightly older looking than when Conan had last set eyes on him five years before—Conan reckoned he must be fifty now. He was a thin as a rail. As usual, he was dressed in a good quality blue blazer and gray slacks. As Houghton drew closer to the door Conan saw that he was wearing the gold badge of the Southern Counties Ocean Cruising Club on the breast pocket of the blazer. Houghton's wavy brown hair was, he saw, now graying over the ears. His skin was pallid. He wore dark sunglasses. Conan wondered if Houghton's eyesight was any worse. Houghton had lost one eye and damaged the other when a mainsail boom had smashed him. It had been during a transatlantic solo race. Houghton had been damned lucky to be sighted by a freighter which, seeing his sails flapping wildly, had rescued him after he had been two days unconscious on deck, prevented from falling overboard only by the fallen, loose mainsail. He was pleased that he had not mentioned Houghton's half-blindness to Ruth. It would have only made her worry the more . . .

Houghton was shaking his hand. He was taller than Conan by two inches. His voice was high, and his accent was pure Cambridge. To Conan, after four years' sojourn among New York accents, Houghton's voice sounded, at first, a little effusive but he dismissed that thought quickly from his mind. There had never been a tougher nut than Houghton in his sailing days. Never, anywhere.

The fact that it was rumored that Houghton preferred men to women was neither here nor there, Conan reflected. There had never been a breath of scandal about him where his crews were concerned and for Conan, as for most ocean roamers, what Houghton did ashore was his own concern. His semiblindness must be cramping his style, poor devil, was Conan's only thought about it.

Houghton greeted him, "Bill Conan! Hullo old chap! How *are* you?" He glanced at the newspaper Conan had tucked under his arm. "Ah, see you've been weighing up the competition, eh?"

"Mike, good to see you. Yes, it's quite a lineup, isn't it?" Conan took one of the club race-coordinator's small cases from him, held his elbow, and guided him toward the taxi rank. "Do you mind if we call at my pension? I want to collect my things. We can have a spot of lunch there, too, before we go over to *Josephine*," he explained.

They reached the cab rank and stood waiting for the line of passengers to slowly move along. It was the only place in Portugal that Conan had ever seen a queue. Usually it was everyone for himself and the devil take the hindmost. He turned to Houghton. "Bad luck about poor old Shaughnessy."

Houghton peered at him through his dark glasses. "Yes, an awful shame. Julia—did you meet his wife?"

Conan shook his head. Then remembering that Houghton might not be able to see him clearly, he said, "No."

"She took it very badly . . . still in hospital for shock . . ."

"I can't recall, did he have any children?" Conan asked.

"Yes, two. One of school age. The Royal Air Force—he used to be in the air force you know."

Conan hesitated, then said, "No, I didn't, he never mentioned it to me . . . oh, yes, he—I remember seeing the R.A.F. ensign on *Josephine* in Annapolis."

Houghton continued, "The Air Force Benevolent Association are taking care of the school expenses, at least for this year."

There was silence between them until Conan said quietly, "What a stupid way for a man like Shaughnessy to go—in a car accident, of all things."

"Yes, he flew back from here for yet another inquiry into the Fastnet fiasco. He was on his way back to Heathrow Airport. . . . I rather think he would have been happier going some other—" Houghton stopped himself, leaving the sentence unfinished. They both could end it themselves. They both, in the brilliant Lisbon sunshine, had momentary visions of fierce, angry, black seas overwhelming them. Conan mentally shook himself free of the nightmarish image. They had both stared death in the face more times than they cared to remember, yet they both knew that under the threat of imminent death is the closest a man gets to absolute freedom. They also both knew how, when death is surveyed at close quarters, a little too close, the imagination can come into its own, and that if a man yields to it his emotions can take on an intensity, a depth, that while clarifying the reasons for life, tend to obscure the means of staying alive. They were terribly British about it; they pragmatically stowed the thoughts of death away in the nethermost lockers of their minds. Death and taxes are always with the Americans—to these eternal banes the British customarily add a third, all their own, the weather.

"Looks like we'll have fine weather, anyway," Conan observed, "for the start."

Houghton inspected the sky briefly. "Beautiful, gorgeous day," he agreed.

It was their turn for a cab. Managing to look officious and servile at the same time, the airport cab-regulator ordered up a car with an imperious bark, and bowed and scraped as Conan pressed a five escudo note into his hand for justifying his existence.

As the cab accelerated Houghton said, "Aw'fly glad to get your telegram. We were worried stiff. No one else, at least no one we could get hold of in time, was qualified by the thousand-mile solo trip, you see. If we'd found anyone who stood a chance it would have meant they'd have had to take *Josephine* out immediately—last week d'you see—and sail around like the dickens for a week or so to get the thousand miles under their belt, then come back into Lisbon and immediately depart for the race. What with all the stores and last minute checkups it would have been absolutely impossible, d'you see, Bill?"

"What about Tim Sharples? I heard he sailed back from Capetown months ago."

"He did, but he's delivering a sixty-footer for some Continental bigwig—Holland to Rio. Took off three weeks ago."

"Who's sponsoring *Josephine*, anyway?" asked Conan.

"The British Paper Industries."

"God, don't tell me she's made of reinforced papier-mâché!"

Houghton laughed and slapped his knee. "Same old Conan," he guffawed. "No, regular Fiberglas, all built under Lloyd's supervision, of course, three inch by the keel and all that. She's an aw'fly good vessel, Bill, take anything thrown her. She took quite a beating in the Round Britain race and in the Fastnet last year . . . came through with hardly a scratch . . . solid as the Rock of Gibraltar . . . but you know her . . ."

A vision flashed through Conan's mind of the miles of tunnel which honeycomb Gibraltar, but all he said was yes.

Houghton continued, speaking softly as he stared through the cab window at the scenery they were passing. "We stored her for fourteen months. There's everything . . . oodles of food cans, labels all stripped off and the contents marked with paint, of course . . . and freeze-dried foods . . . the food companies did us proud."

"Side band radio?" asked Conan. "Auxiliary generator?"

"The best—I can't recall the details, but you'll see when we get aboard." Houghton lit a cigarette. "Shaughnessy stripped just about everything from the accommodation, of course. He was a ruthless devil when it came to saving weight, but you'll see for yourself. And by the way . . ." Houghton tapped his knee "you'd better check as much as you can as soon as possible—we've only three working days until the start of the race. I'm sorry, I'm afraid it's something of a pierhead jump for you, Bill." They were silent as the cab stopped at a light. Then, as they shot forward again Houghton said, "But anyway, if I know—knew Shaughnessy, he left everything shipshape, in apple-pie order."

Conan thought that would make an odd epitaph. He envisaged the legend carved into a stone cross set into the green sward atop a sea-beaten cliff in Donegal: "*Sean Shaughnessy—1930–1980—he left everything shipshape and in apple-pie order.*" He dismissed the sacrilegious image from his mind as the cab came to a halt outside the Pension Coimbra-Madrid.

They sat down to lunch at Conan's regular table on the pavement outside the Pastilleria Suisse. Houghton offered to treat Conan, who, taking advantage of a rare occasion, ordered sauerkraut with apples and beer, *bife a Portuguesa*—an eight-ounce steak, sautéed in garlic with a thick slice of ham on top—and a *Barriga de Freira*, a chocolate pudding. "Might as well fill up now," he said to Houghton, as the waiter took his order. Houghton ordered *Carne de Porco com Ameijoas*—pork with clams, on Conan's recommendation. "I'd have it myself if seafood agreed with my stomach," he told the race coordinator. For wine, Conan, at Houghton's invitation, chose a fine *vinho verde* which the coordinator, who had a sensitive palate, acclaimed. They ate leisurely, discussing at first the many British influences in Lisbon. Houghton remarked on the green double-decker buses and the red British-style free-standing, upright cylindrical mailboxes. "Yes, you can get genuine ginger beer and a good cup of tea here, too," commented Conan, half-sarcastically. "And the London papers, of course," he added.

As the waiter brought after-lunch coffees, Conan leaned across to Houghton, who sat pensively watching the passersby on the sidewalk. "Mike," he said, "this Fastnet race disaster—what was it all about? I've been rather shut away in New York and only heard and saw a few obviously garbled reports on the radio and TV."

Houghton looked at him in surprise. "I should have thought that you, of all people, would have found out as much as possible about it," he said. He could be unctuous when he wanted to be. "I believe the *New York Times* reported it, and the American yachting magazines." He flicked some cigarette ash from his blazer. "But I suppose that now you're a *writer*—" Houghton pressed his chin into his neck and pursed his lips.

Conan did not let him finish. "I was writing my first novel," he said. "It took me eight months. I live like a bloody hermit when I'm writing, Mike—all I do is write, eat, keep off booze, and sleep. I had a deadline on *The Flying Dutchman*, and, well, I just didn't see anything about the Fastnet."

"Of course, old man, I understand," said Houghton. He lit a cigarette. "What happened, very briefly, is this. It wasn't exactly a fiasco; more aw'fly bad luck. Just over three hundred yachts—three hundred and three, to be precise—left Falmouth, the starting point, in August, for the usual course: out across the Irish Sea, around Fastnet rock, and back to Falmouth. They were mostly well into the middle of the Celtic Sea, as you know a roughish spot at the best of times, when suddenly, virtually without warning, gale force winds generated, it turned out, by a rapidly deepening low pressure area, struck the fleet. The wind rose to Force Eleven and the seas steepened until they were forty to forty-four feet high; quite a dusting, you see, Bill."

"Mmm," said Conan. "Quite a dusting." He inwardly smiled at the understatement. Force Eleven is just under hurricane strength.

"There was the devil to pay. One hundred and twelve boats were knocked over on their beam ends to the horizontal..." Houghton's brow knitted as he recalled the figures "and seventy-seven of those were blown over *beyond* the horizontal. Five of the boats reported that they spent between thirty seconds and five minutes totally inverted—upside down in the sea. Fifty-one vessels reported that one or more crew members were washed overboard. Of these, several went overboard more than once. Twenty-six boats reported a safety harness failure. Of the fifteen men in all who died during or as a result of the storm, six died after their safety harness, or a safety harness attachment point, failed. Seven more of the dead were lost in incidents involving life rafts..." A pained look crossed Houghton's face. "You can guess what happened...."

Conan nodded slowly. "I think so. The yachts they abandoned were afterward found safely afloat."

"Exactly, each and every yacht was recovered. If those people had only stayed on board their yachts they would have very probably, all of them, been still alive today."

"The old story," commented Conan. "It sounds like a massacre. Tell me, Mike, were there many inexperienced skippers out there? I suppose there must have been. There's not much of a qualification requirement for the Fastnet, is there?"

A sudden gust of wind blew along the Rossio, sending a peasant woman's wide straw hat flying. There was a honk of horns and squeals of brakes as cars swerved to avoid the half-dozen men, idlers and hucksters, who ran and scrambled to retrieve the hat as it rolled away across the wide square. The woman, a basket of tomatoes at her feet, stood, arms angled, hands on her wide hips, her face red with the sun and the excitement of the city. Conan and Houghton watched, intrigued, as a one-armed bootblack, with grave courtesy, handed the woman back her headgear.

Houghton returned to the subject of the disaster. "That's a moot point. The main board of inquiry did not think that experience or lack of it had a great deal of bearing on the number of knockdowns, the amount of severe damage, abandonments, or loss of life. I personally disagree with them on the latter two, the desertions and deaths, and I think you'll agree with me, Bill, that few experienced skippers would allow their crew to abandon a vessel that is still watertight to a degree, still afloat?"

"Bloody right. They should have stuck to their vessels. If she'll float for an hour she'll float for a day, as the old saying has it, and God knows, even a vessel hull down and leaking like a sieve is safer than any life raft in seas that big."

"Quite," said Houghton.

"What happened to the BBC, I mean the weather forecasts?"

"Those who listened in got three hours' warning of the gale. Most of the boats could not receive the VHF and Coast Radio forecasts. You know the Western Approaches, Bill, how rapidly a storm can brew up with hardly any warning."

"How many did you say were lost through safety harness failure?" asked Conan.

"Six," Houghton sighed. "I'm glad you brought that up, because the RORC recommended that double harness be worn in severe conditions, so I've brought you an extra harness along—you already have two on board, of course."

"I appreciate it," said Conan.

"They also pointed out the danger of clipping the harness line onto the vessel's standing lifelines, and they recommend an adequte deck line from the cockpit to points forward in the boat, to clip the harness line to."

"I do that anyway."

"I'll discuss the life raft, life jacket, and pyrotechnics with you tomorrow, Bill. I know you'll ask what's the point when your course will mainly be over such empty spaces of the ocean, but there might be a chance of collision in a shipping lane, that kind of thing—"

"Cheerful today, Mike," Conan murmured.

"Well, you never know, nice to be on the safe side . . ." As he paid the check, Houghton left the rest unsaid.

Houghton, at this moment, actually envied Conan because he knew that the more one lives life the less one fears death. It was only when drumming away on a close reach or winging on a dead run out in the ocean that he had ever really lived life and forgotten the shadow of eventual death. His continual disappointments in love had been so many that now Houghton accepted it as a rather unpleasant necessity. He no longer looked for a meaning to life in that direction, and as a poor substitute (he could no longer skipper a boat), threw himself into his work with an intensity that amazed everyone who knew him. It was sad, but true, Houghton reflected, if we don't love we don't live fully—and if we don't live fully then we fear death all the more. He knew the paradox that it is only by loving that we come to realize the full import of death. Houghton envied the Scot, too, because death must now be always with Conan, near the surface of his consciousness, bringing stark contrast to the brilliant colors of life in all their glory, enabling him to savor every breath, every drop, every morsel, every sight, every sound, every emotion; more than anyone who has not lived with death could ever know.

For Conan it was different. He always lived life—really lived life—even in his writing, fully, *all stops out and damn the torpedoes!*

Conan collected his duffel bag from the floor and strode to the edge of the sidewalk to hail a cab. Houghton joined him. Conan studied him for a minute, then grinned widely. Houghton looked at him quizzically. Conan, his eyes briefly following the motion of a passing woman, said, "Yes, like you say, Mike, it really is nice to be on the safe side."

As a taxi drew up, they both piled inside, chuckling softly at the subtlety of the allusion.

"Club Nautico de Belém," Conan ordered the driver, as the cab, horn honking, shot off into the traffic.

They were silent on the way to Belém, but both of them knew what the other was thinking of . . . the thirty thousand miles of wind-swept, heaving, empty ocean and the months of effort and struggle that lay between Bill Conan and victory.

As they overtook the Lisbon-Belém train, Conan remembered being with Ruth the day before. He was still thinking of Ruth when they arrived on the jetty. He felt deprived. Her leaving had left a void in part of him. He was aware of his own conceits, his own egotism, but he knew that loving Ruth, missing her, was his own salvation.

"She's a beauty!" Houghton exclaimed, looking down at *Josephine*, as if it were not the fiftieth time he had gazed on the boat.

"She surely is," Conan said, as he clambered out lugging his duffel bag, not thinking at all, yet, of *Josephine*. "She surely is!"

Chapter 5

"THANK GOD SHAUGHNESSY had good musical taste, anyway," Conan remarked to Houghton who, with the ship's checklist held close to his failing eye under the main cabin lamp, was marking off items as Conan called them out. The list was thirty-five pages long. There were a total of 1,754 items on the list. This was apart from the engine and generator spares lists.

"Tape cassettes—thirty-five in all." Conan called out. "Debussy—Vivaldi—Ravel—Brahms—Mendelssohn—*The Hebrides Overture*—Beethoven—Chopin—Bach—Tchaikovsky, 1812—great stuff in dirty weather." Conan crouched to read labels on the plastic boxes under the coach roof. "*Tannhäuser, Ride of the Valkyries,* and here's Gilbert and Sullivan—*The Mikado, The Pirates of Penzance,* and . . . well, well, good old Sean, I never knew he was a jazz buff—Bix Beiderbecke, Fats Waller—Jelly Roll Morton . . . and . . . hello, what's this? . . . Noel Coward . . . 'Selection including "Don't put your daughter on the stage Mrs. . . . Worthington" '?"

"I gave that to Julia . . . his wife . . . to present to him. Thought it might amuse him," asserted Houghton sadly.

"Well, that's about it for today," declared Conan. They had started the inventory—checking the manifest, they called it—as soon as they had boarded *Josephine* and stowed their gear below. In the bright afternoon sunlight, Conan had carefully checked all the rigging, the cables, and the turnbuckles. They had rigged the bosun's chair and he had gone up to the masthead and worked his way down, carefully examining the radar reflector, every block, the spreaders, every tang, every toggle, every clevis pin, every inch of the mast and the standing and running rigging. Then, working his way forward from the stern, Conan had inspected the self-steering gear, the backstay adjusters and insulators, the booms, the bales, the claws, the vangs, the goosenecks on the mainmast, the lifelines, their stanchions and their fixings, above deck and below, the sheet and halyard winches—great, self-tailing beauties from Barlow—all the cleats, fairleads, sail tracks, sheet stoppers, sail slides, the reefing gear on the main, every shackle, the navigation lights; in short he went over the deck and sailing gear as carefully as would any skipper worth his salt, who held his life in his own hands.

As he made the topside inspection, and gazed over the sleek deck, the smooth lines, and *Josephine*'s heavy chrome fittings, Conan wryly thought to himself what a change had been wrought in small craft over the past three decades. He remembered some of the craft he had picked up and commissioned years ago. They were mostly wood. Some of them fifty or sixty years old, fastened with iron. Headed for the tropics they were the prospective feeding grounds of the teredo worm, an unpleasant creature that inhabits tropical waters and that can reduce a wooden vessel to the watertight integrity of Gruyère within months. The teredo, he remembered, has a head shaped like a metal drill, and about as hard. The teredo would make a pinhole in a plank, work its way in, then, still a tiny animal, it would turn at right angles and attack the length of the plank, eating its way through the wood until the plank was, in a few weeks, riddled right through, but treacherously; outside the plank there would be no sign of the teredo worm's depredations. To repel the teredo worm, boat's bottoms had been sheathed in copper. But nothing was easy or as simple as it looked on wooden ships. If the bottom was copper covered and the fastenings of the vessel were of iron, then galvanic action would set up, the iron would be eaten away, and in a year or two the boat's planks would be falling apart.

On arrival in the tropics, he, sometimes alone, sometimes with a crew, would careen the boat, that is, lay her over at low tide on a beach or in a mosquito-infested mangrove swamp, and inspect the bottom for minute holes. Nine out of ten times they found, after hot and heavy work scraping the bottom clean, it would be holed in a hundred places. They used to burn the bottom planks with a blowtorch to bring the worms, long now and fat, squirming out of their holes. Then they left the hull heeled over for a few days. This was, by tradition, supposed to kill what worms were left. Then they keeled the boat over on her other side and started three days' work on that. *Josephine* was Fiberglas. There would be no teredos in her, ever; blood, tears, anxiety, and sweat maybe—but no teredo.

Down below again, as the sun eased its way over the spreader, Conan checked the two full sets of spare sails and the three storm jibs and the three trysails—again carefully, for the heavy weather sails must be the best on board, "like a whorehouse madam, a vessel only wears her best clothes when the going gets rough," as Conan put it to Houghton, who wrinkled his nose slightly, then snorted a short laugh of agreement.

Next Conan, working his way back through what Houghton called "the rather Spartan" main cabin—the table had been stripped out by Shaughnessy—he checked the mast step in the bilge and the bilges themselves. As he did so, he wondered what Houghton would have thought of the Arab dhow he had once taken over in Egypt and delivered to a mad British army colonel in Malta. It was twenty-one years before—in 1960. When Conan had first boarded the dhow the two Arab crew had been hauling up clear water from her bilge well. They had bailed her out all the five days they had waited for permission from the authorities to leave port, and all the two weeks' sail to Malta. Of all the dhows that had been in Alexandria she was the smallest, dirtiest, and smelliest. She had no accommodation at all and there was always short rations. The only thing that kept the sea from swamping her, once they were on passage, was a loosely woven palm-leaf matting which they had lashed to her bulwarks. She was fast, graceful, with good lines, but she was one of the most God-awful craft he had ever sailed in. Her high mainmast, riggingless and raked sharply forward, seemed to have sprouted out of the hull. The lateen yards, all of fifty feet long, were made of two tree branches tied together, her cordage was homemade from coconut fiber and her sails had been run up by the ex-owner's wife, patiently, from cheap number six Egyptian cotton.

They had worn into Valetta thin, thirsty, and half-dead from bailing continuously, and the mad colonel had accused them of malingering. They were a day later than Conan had estimated in his letter to the colonel.

Conan smiled as he lit the alcohol pressure stove and oven in the galley. "Might as well make hay while the sun shines," he said as he made tea for Houghton and himself.

The engine was a straightforward Perkins 41 horsepower diesel. He browsed through the operator's manual, checked the engine's holding down bolts and oil level, saw that it was charging the batteries and that the ahead and astern gear were functioning, then stopped the main engine—it would be used little, if at all, on the race—and turned his attention to the auxiliary generator, another Perkins, a 15-kw diesel. With this he would charge his four batteries daily with enough electricity to operate the radio twice daily, and give him the small amount of light he would need for navigation and domestic purposes.

"I'll go over the side in the morning and check the through-hull fittings and propellor, and give her a bit of a scrub," Conan told Houghton, after he had checked the fuel and the water tanks. All full.

Next Conan checked the navigational gear, the two sextants, the walnut-boxed chronometer, the navigational tables and nautical almanac, and a hundred charts—a few ocean charts and one for every major port near the race route, in case *Josephine* might have to abandon the race and make for safe haven. "One hundred and five pencils," Conan called out, as he completed the navigational stock-taking.

He recalled the time he had sighted a little twenty-foot sloop way out in mid-Atlantic, between the Canary Islands and Barbados. The small, scruffy boat had hailed his thirty-footer, and he had gone close to her and heaved to. The lone sailor was a young Swiss, anxious to know his whereabouts. Conan had told him, and then asked if he needed anything else, and how was he navigating? The Swiss youth, Ronnie by name, had waved an ordinary household atlas at him, then opened to the page showing the Atlantic Ocean and indicated to him a red pencil line scratched out on the map. As far as he could find out, Ronnie never did reach Barbados. It had been late June. There had been a hurricane only a few days later. . . . Conan frowned and turned back to the job in hand.

By the time the electronics—the anemometer, wind direction indicator, wind speed indicator, knot meter, depth-sounder, the Loran, and radio transmitter-receiver (the finest, from Denmark)—had been checked out, it was well past suppertime. Wearily, they made their way up the companionway to the cockpit. They were aware of movement and voices on the other race vessels each side of *Josephine*.

"Well, what do you think of her, Bill?" asked Houghton.

"She'll do."

"We'll go through the food list tomorrow afternoon. Sean took in fourteen months' supply—a lot of freeze-dried stuff well sealed up, steaks and all that." Houghton handed Conan the keys to *Josephine*. It was a very British ceremony. It was now official; Conan was now skipper of *Josephine*.

"Cheers, Mike," Conan acknowledged, and bent to lock the hatch door. As he straightened up again Conan said, "Sad, that last entry in the log by Shaughnessy before he left the boat."

"Oh?"

"Yes, he wrote 'a very fine, sea-kindly vessel and I have every confidence in making a good show in the coming months.' "

"Poor old—" Houghton did not finish the sentence. A voice calling from the jetty high above them interrupted.

"Ahoy, *Josephine*!"

"Be right up, we're coming ashore!" Conan shouted. He looked up and saw a figure silhouetted in one of the yellow-orange pools of light that streamed from the dockside lamps. Holding on to the boat's mooring lines, they made their way up the sea-moss covered sloping jetty wall, Houghton first, with Conan close behind him. They pulled themselves onto the quay. In the clear, star-laden sky a three-quarter moon was suspended over the gigantic granite memorial to Prince Henry the Navigator which overlooks the Tagus River close by the yacht basin.

The figure on the quay approached them. Soon Conan saw that it was that of a tall, slim young man wearing a baseball cap. The young man smiled, showing a perfect set of teeth in the lamplight, and stretched out his hand. "Jack Hanson, *Sundance Kid*," he drawled in a loud voice. "Real pleased to meet you dudes. Which one of you is Bill Conan?"

"The man himself," replied Conan, putting out his hand.

"Wow," shouted Hanson, "this's really something . . . there was a rumor goin' around you were here . . . I'm an avid reader of your stuff . . . you really laid a trip on me, man!" He was dressed casually, in an old brown sweater and blue jeans and running shoes. Under his long-peaked baseball cap his hair was dirty blond and so long it was almost down to his shoulders. He wore a pair of rimless half-glasses low down on his short nose, and a beard so stringy and fair that at first Conan did not see it.

"This is Mike Houghton. He's race-coordinator of the Southern Counties Ocean Cruising—"

Hanson didn't let Conan finish. He grabbed Houghton's hand. "Say, you're not the Mike Houghton that won the Capetown-Perth 71?" he shouted.

"Actually, yes," murmured Houghton, somewhat abashed.

"Yeah . . . read the account in . . . some magazine. Say, that was some tough trip, huh, Mike?" Hanson's voice reminded Conan of a foghorn.

"Quite boisterous." Houghton peered at Hanson, trying to see him in the dim lamplight. Three of the five boats that had competed in the race had disappeared without trace in the angry Southern Ocean.

"Were you in the last Fastnet race?" Hanson shouted at Houghton. Then, without waiting for a reply, in a rush of words he addressed Conan. "I know *you* weren't . . . I saw you on the Geoff Muffin show last August . . . hell, I wish I'd known you'd be out in California, I live only a few blocks away from Geoff's studio . . ."

Houghton said, his voice cutting softly through the shadows, "We're just off to eat. Have you—?"

"Hell no, I been out joggin' . . . I run ten miles a day . . . ashore."

"Why don't you come with us?" Houghton offered. "We're only going for something simple at one of the local places over in the village."

"Can I? Wow, ain't that somethin'? Me going to dinner with Bill Conan and Mike Houghton." Hanson nodded over his shoulder at the other racing boats. "The others . . . well, the two Brits keep pretty much to themselves. The Aussie's taken up with the chick from New Zealand, and the Frenchman Duplessis and the Swede, Larsen, both have their wives here. There's only the Polish guy left on his own, and his English is . . . zip." He grinned. "Pete, that's the Polish guy, he's real cool, though. Ballin' a chick from the harbor master's office."

"Good bloke, eh?" Conan interpreted for Houghton, whose brow was furrowing in puzzlement at Hanson's brand of English.

"Really," murmured Hanson, his voice, for the first time, low and normal. "First foreign commie I ever met . . . but maybe he isn't . . . but if they let him go like this . . . ?"

They walked through the park, past the swan pool now bathed in moonlight. Conan recalled being there with Ruth only yesterday afternoon in the sunshine. He quickened his pace to escape from the recollection. It was too painful, too soon after her leaving.

The cafe on Belém's main street was plain and garishly lit with fluorescent lamps, which cast a cold, pallid glare over the table. They were served a simple meal of local ham—rather tough, bitter, and dry to their tastes—eggs, and beans, which they eased down with a good bottle of *vinho verde.*

While Houghton silently listened, Conan and the young American discussed various aspects of their respective vessels and the coming race.

"*Sundance Kid* sounds like a first-class boat," concluded Conan, after Hanson had enumerated her equipment, all the latest, up-to-date, "state-of-the-art" gear.

"I ain't sweatin'. It's going to take some real downers for me to cop out. It—she was cool in the Bay of Biscay, and that was rough weather, man."

"How did you get into this, Jack?" Houghton asked Hanson quietly.

Hanson's voice echoed around the room. "Oh . . . I was doin' my thing . . . surfin' an' dinghy racin' and all that stuff, out in Long Beach, and this dude Cooley comes out from nowhere and like socks it to me . . . I'm tellin' you, he just zonked me down flat ... it was *far out* ... he just comes up to me an' asks like if I could get into it. He's gotten the A.C.H. and the I.P.P. and three other of those fat-cat companies puttin' up the green. When I asked him why he was layin' this on me he said"—Hanson grinned hugely—"it was 'cos they wanted like an all-out all-American boy out there. So I said okay, but whattam I gonna do in the meanwhile—this was the beginnin' of last year, see?—I was like at college an' stuff an' he got them to lay five hundred bucks a month on me as a retainer, see?" Hanson had a way of leaning back, his eyebrows raised, his pale blue eyes wide open, staring to see the effect of his words on whomever he talked at.

"Good deal," remarked Conan, smiling at the American.

"Astonishingly good," agreed Houghton.

Hanson continued, "If I win I pay 'em back, but if not I'm like still on the five hundred charlies a month until the end of the race, see?" He leaned back again, eyes wide open, looking over his half-glasses at Conan.

"How will they cover the expenditures?" asked Houghton.

"I've already filmed eight commercials for stuff supplied to the boat, like each one was filmed twice, one version for if I win and one for if not. Cooley's a real hotshot manager."

"That's what we used to call covering your yardarm," Conan asserted.

Hanson turned to him and beamed over his half-glasses. His light blue eyes twinkled. "Hey, I dig that," he said.

"What does Cooley get out of it?" Houghton asked Hanson.

"The sponsors, Cooley, and me split three ways if I win."

"Fair enough," observed Houghton, "but Conan's on a better deal. If he wins he keeps the lot, lucky devil."

They drank their coffees in silence until Hanson demanded, "Say, you guys been to the Maritime Museum just up the road? The Aussie—what's he called?—Hunt ... yeah, Paddy Hunt, was telling me like it's quite a trip ... really something. He says it's like one of the best in the world."

"It is, I know it well," agreed Conan. "I'll show you round, if you'd like to come, on ... let's see, we're going to be bloody busy tomorrow and Tuesday scrubbing the bottom, checking out the last items in the boat, and the Yacht Club reception in the evening ... make it Wednesday, in the afternoon, eh, Jack? We should be all on top line for the off by then."

Houghton interjected, "Make it Thursday morning, Bill, my flight is in the early afternoon and I would like to come with you. There are some portalanos I want to see ..." He saw Hanson's brow knit. "They are ancient sea charts. I've been reading Charles Hapgood—he's one of your people, you know, American professor. He's written a book, *Maps of the Ancient Sea Kings*. You really ought to read it some time. Very intriguing. He postulates that the earth's coasts and oceans were mapped—charted—thousands of years before Christ ... and the Piri Re'is map"—Houghton tapped a cup with a spoon to stress his point—". . . dated 1512, mark you, was the direct descendant of charts made by the ancient sea-peoples of Atlantis."

"Atlantis, wow!" exclaimed Hanson. His voice rocked the room.

"Quite," said Houghton, as Conan, grinning, watched him and listened intently. "The Turkish Admiral Piri Re'is must have had something to work from when he drew quite accurate maps of the coasts of western South America and Africa and—and this is the strangest thing—of the coasts of Greenland and Antarctica before they were covered by ice ... and now, using modern detection instruments, which can measure under the ice, we've found that the coast of Queen Maud Land, Antarctica, is pretty near as it's depicted by Piri Re'is. Very strange indeed. Perhaps there's something in it ..."

"Atlantis—what about Atlantis?" Hanson eagerly asked.

"Hapgood suggests that it was in the central, equatorial Atlantic," Houghton replied, "between the closest parts of Africa and South America, somewhere around where St. Paul's Rocks now are. He also suggests that the ancient Sea Kings of Atlantis colonized Crete and Cyprus and Egypt ... and even this area around Lisbon, before the great disaster, whatever it was, which destroyed Atlantis."

"Wow, like race memories of the Flood," exclaimed Hanson.

"Quite," Houghton agreed. "But look here"—he signalled the cafe owner for the check—"I don't know about you chaps, but I'm bone weary. Got up at five A.M. to catch my plane. I think we ought to ..." He turned to Hanson and smiled as he hesitated. "What is it you fellows say? Hit the sack?"

"Crash, flake out," replied the American.

Conan asked, "Do you use those terms now?"

"Yeah."

"That's funny. We used to use exactly the same expressions in the Andrew years ago."

Hanson looked puzzled. "The *what*?"

"Bill means the Royal Navy," explained Houghton, as they left the cafe to walk back to the boats.

Hanson turned to Houghton and looked at him for a long moment. Then he exclaimed, quietly, in an awed tone, "Atlantis ... wow?" and, grinning, shook his head and hair for a minute in semidisbelief.

Conan said jocosely, "Mike's got a bee in his bonnet about ancient voyages. He believes that the world, the oceans, rather, were once ruled by a great race of mariners who were based on the legendary island-continent of Atlantis. That's the theory, right, Mike?"

They were passing again through the waterfront park. The moon hung silver over the black-shining estuary of the Tagus, away in the west. The stars in their constellations trailed after her.

"I don't *believe* it," replied Houghton, "but I do think it is highly possible that such a culture did exist . . . and that somehow their civilization came to an end through some great disaster. Who knows? It might have been caused by a nuclear accident, it might have been the ice melting at the retreat of an ice age raising the levels of the oceans. . . . Who can tell? But there is evidence, as I've discussed, that points to the existence of people who knew how to map the coasts of the world accurately thousands of years ago."

"Wow, wouldn't it be something if we could like trace them?" interjected Hanson. "Maybe we could find out how to avoid a similar disaster . . . maybe they were, well, just anything . . . like in touch with nature much more close than we are. It freaks me out!"

"Yes, it is intriguing, isn't it?" murmured Houghton. "What do you think, Bill?"

"Sounds a bit like *Alice in Wonderland* to me. I'll believe it when I see positive proof."

"Same old Bill," observed Houghton.

"I suppose there could be something in it, Mike," retorted Conan, "but we get so much . . . escapism, I mean in books and films, nowadays. Look at all the fanciful gubbins that's hurled at the public these days, flying saucers and space wars, and all that damned claptrap about the Bermuda Triangle and paranoia-peddling piffle about man-eating sharks. Look, I've just spent four years having this bullshit hurled about around me, Mike. There's big money in it—at least if the people who churn it out are to be believed—who knows? Who can believe anything they say? All I know is that I'm fed up to the gills with sensationalism." Conan almost tripped over a mooring line on the edge of the dock. Houghton, although half-blind, sensed him stagger and quickly grabbed his elbow.

"It's as if they need a substitution for the God they no longer believe in," Conan continued, as he recovered his balance. "It's as if they have to have little green men with superior intelligence out there who are going to come down among them and save them from themselves . . ."

Houghton rejoined, "Or as if, in order to escape from the pointlessness of their daily life, the alienation, they feel that they must be fed horror. One more pain to dull the existing agony . . . frustration, I suppose."

"I think they take it because they dig it. They like it," suggested Hanson. "Johnny Do-right is a funny guy . . . freaky, at least out on the Coast."

"From what I saw in my time ashore," Conan observed, "it's because they're so out of touch with nature and the natural world—how many people do you see, for example, in New York, ever looking up at the sky at night?"

"Or even in the day, I guess," agreed the American.

Conan said, "Many of them have been so dulled by all the barrage of crap flung at them day and night . . . then to insulate themselves they get wrapped up in themselves." They were above the vessels now. "Oh—what the hell—g'night, Jack!" Conan helped Houghton over the rail and placed himself below him, so he could be guided down in the dark.

"Yeah, see you guys at the reception tomorrow," came back the stentorian voice of the young American as he disappeared into the shadows in the direction of his own craft.

"You take the pit, Mike, I'll sleep up on deck." Conan unlocked the hatch door. "Pass me up a blanket, will you. There's a spare one under the berth."

"Young Hanson's a bit of a character, eh, Mike?" Conan commented with a grin. "Enthusiastic, I'd say."

"Can't imagine sailing with him," rejoined Houghton gruffly. "I'd need bally earplugs!"

"He'd be handy in a fog on a lee shore," joked Conan.

"Or in an argument with one of those dratted Turkish customs officers," said Houghton, chuckling. "It's true what someone said, you know, Bill, about American conversation as opposed to English . . . British." Houghton remembered Conan's Scottish origins.

"What's that?"

"Well, that our conversation is like a tennis match . . . you know . . . I biff and you boff, and it goes back and forth. But these Americans—their conversations are like . . . cycle races, with each one puffing and pedalling and forging ahead on his own bike regardless of anyone else."

"Some of them are quite good at argument," Conan said finally.

"Sleep well, Bill," called Houghton, later, as he laid himself down on the one berth, but Conan was already fast asleep under the dimmed stars.

Chapter 6

THE FOOD AND DRINKS for the race reception were paid for by the *London Globe.* The function was hosted by the Portuguese navy, who donated the use of the Maritime Museum reception hall and the services of the Naval detachments that guarded the museum, a group of personable young men, many of whom spoke English and French.

Before the "flower revolution" of 1974, such functions usually took place in the Yacht Club, but a worker's committee had taken over the operation of the club in 1975, as part of the worker's participation program. This had all been well meant, very idealistic, and finely intended. Initially the program had swung ahead in wild enthusiasm. The former bar steward had taken over the general management and one of the carpenters had been voted into the position of yard manager. The former management had been retired into limbo with a pittance of a pension.

By the end of 1976 it was obvious, at least to mariners, that the new order was not as ideal as it had sounded in the budding of the flower revolution. The former bar steward was drinking himself to death and the carpenter had taken into his employ, or been coerced into taking, half the lay-abouts of the Lisbon waterfront. The club, consequently, had fallen into a steady decline. The former steward had been packed off to an institution by the end of 1977 and the former carpenter had become a figurehead, whose only obvious function was to attend the weekly payment of vastly inflated wages to a vastly inflated staff, most of whom hardly ever appeared at the club except on paydays. Thenceforward, until the general election of 1979 when a conservative government was returned, the deterioration of the club houses and grounds had been accepted by all concerned as one of a growing number of irritating but seemingly, for the time being, inevitable facts of life.

In the spring of 1980 the worker's committee had been dissolved, and now, a year later, the club members and former staff were once more in charge. The first thing they, in their turn, had done when they took over, was discharge a good sixty percent of the "committee," generally retaining those who had worked at the club before the revolution, and who were known not to have been too "revolutionary," which in Portugal meant "wanting something without any effort." The club was still in a state of flux, as Conan put it "with everything like a midshipman's locker—all on top and nothing handy." The only things that still operated efficiently were the half-dozen showers, although the hot water boiler had been out of action for years. It was to these not-too-clean cubicles that Conan and Houghton repaired in the late afternoon on Wednesday, after a long day of checking, checking, checking everything on board *Josephine* that had not been checked the day before.

They arrived at the museum courtyard—it was only a five-minute walk from the boat—at dusk. The museum is right next to the Monastery of San Jerónimos, which was now floodlit a warm golden color. The carvings and statues and gargoyles of the monastery facade stood out in bold relief. Thousands of stone saints, the Virgin and the Lord, all floodlight bathed in golden beams, blessed the procession of very expensive cars which rolled up to the museum—Mercedes-Benzes, Cadillacs, and Rolls-Royces mainly, but with a few Ferraris and Alfa Romeos among them—to bring in them the more nonconformist members of the Lisbon *haute monde*.

Houghton was in his navy blue blazer and slacks, which he had carefully brushed down before stepping ashore. Conan was still in his customary light brown corduroys, but, as a concession to the social occasion, he had put on a clean light blue shirt and the Southern Counties Ocean Cruising Club tie. The tie was worn and shiny. The last time he had donned it had been in Falmouth for the party before the start of the 1976 transatlantic race. Ruth has insisted that he take it along. It was the only thing he had rescued from *Hobson's Choice*. He'd been wearing it as a belt.

They skirted around a large group of newly arrived guests, all laughing and greeting each other—the men in black tie and loud, the women in long ball gowns and sedate—and entered the museum main entrance. In the foyer they were received—challenged—by three husky Portuguese seamen. Houghton was busy explaining who they were when an English voice cut through the hubbub.

"Mike! Mike Houghton, good to see you again!" Conan saw a medium height fat man with long sideburns, a red face, and a loud tie grasp Houghton's hand. As he did so the fat man beamed at Conan. "Ah-ha," he exclaimed. "This must be . . . Phil . . . Will . . . Conan?"

"Bill," said Conan.

"Yes, of course," said the fat man. They shook hands cursorily.

Houghton intervened. "Bill Conan, this is Jeremy Findlay of the *Globe.*" He turned to Findlay. "You must be here to cover the start?"

Conan reflected to himself how Houghton was a great one for stating the obvious when he was bored. Houghton had told him how he dreaded these occasions. "It's like playing someone else's record collection for the umpteenth time."

"Everything on top line, old chap?" Findlay addressed Houghton.

"All ready for the off."

Findlay turned to Conan. "All the rum stowed away in the bilge, nice and safe, eh . . . got to look after the bubbly, eh, Conan?"

Conan distrusted journalists. He'd had too many run-ins with them, found too many of their accounts distorted, sometimes hurtfully. Some of the press had blamed, by innuendo, the *Hobson's Choice* episode on drink. He took an immediate dislike to Findlay. "I wrapped all the bottles up in old copies of the *Globe,*" he retorted.

Findlay glanced at him from under lowered brows. His smile stiffened. "Good idea," he said in a low voice. The fat man turned again to Houghton. "Find your way in, Mike. I'm waiting for the Polish chap. . . ."

They were accosted inside the glass doors by a young, very good-looking Portuguese naval cadet, who swept his eyes over Conan's glowering face and corduroys, then at Houghton's nautical blazer and distinguished mien. In excellent English he addressed Houghton in a high, piping voice. "Good evening, sir. May I see your entrance cards, please?"

Houghton handed the cadet their invitations and, his curiosity—and perhaps libido, thought Conan—aroused, leaned forward so as to see more clearly, through his dark glasses, who was behind the voice.

"Ah, Mister Conan," said the cadet, grasping Houghton by the elbow, "come this was please. The captains are all over 'ere, to meet the gentlemen an' the ladies."